{ THE VIEW FROM THE TOP }

{ THE VIEW FROM THE TOP }

hillary frank

· Dutton Books ·

An imprint of Penguin Group (USA) Inc.

Dutton Books
A member of Penguin Group (USA) Inc.

Published by the Penguin Group
Penguin Group (USA) Inc., 375 Hudson Street, New York, New York 10014, USA
Penguin Group (Canada), 90 Eglinton Avenue East, Suite 700, Toronto, Ontario, Canada M4P 2Y3 (a
division of Pearson Penguin Canada, Inc.) · Penguin Books Ltd, 80 Strand, London WC2R 0RL, England
Penguin Ireland, 25 St Stephen's Green, Dublin 2, Ireland (a division of Penguin Books Ltd.)· Penguin
Group (Australia), 250 Camberwell Road, Camberwell, Victoria 3124, Australia (a division of Pearson
Australia Group Pty Ltd.) · Penguin Books India Pvt Ltd, 11 Community Centre, Panchsheel Park, New
Delhi - 110 017, India · Penguin Group (NZ), 67 Apollo Drive, Rosedale, North Shore 0632, New Zealand
(a division of Pearson New Zealand Ltd.) · Penguin Books (South Africa) (Pty) Ltd, 24 Sturdee Avenue,
Rosebank, Johannesburg 2196, South Africa Penguin Books Ltd, Registered Offices:
80 Strand, London WC2R 0RL, England

LIBRARY OF CONGRESS CATALOGING-IN-PUBLICATION DATA

Frank, Hillary.
The view from the top / Hillary Frank.—1st ed.   p. cm.
Summary: Anabelle and her fellow high school graduates navigate their way through a
disastrous summer of love and friendship in the small coastal town of Normal, Maine.
ISBN 978-0-525-42241-9 (hardcover)
[1. Intepersonal relations—Fiction. 2. Dating (Social customs)—Fiction.
3. Friendship—Fiction. 4. Family life—Maine—Fiction. 5. Maine—Fiction.] I. Title.
PZ7.F8493Vie 2010   [Fic]—dc22   2009026143

Published in the United States by Dutton Books,
a member of Penguin Group (USA) Inc.
345 Hudson Street, New York, New York 10014
www.penguin.com/youngreaders

Designed by Abby Kuperstock

Printed in USA · First Edition
1   3   5   7   9   10   8   6   4   2

For Jonathan

CONTENTS

{ THE VIEW FROM THE TOP }

{ The **PIANO** *with a* **MISSING TOOTH** }

anabelle seulliere

Of all the weird things about the gift Matt had just given Anabelle, the part that freaked her out most was its beard.

"So I guess you're not planning on shaving for a while?" she asked, holding up the handmade wooden jewelry box with a colorful clay replica of her boyfriend on the front.

"No, I'm keeping it." Matt rubbed the Brillo-pad-ish dark hair on his chin. "It makes me look pensive. Sophisticated."

And old, Anabelle thought, taking in their reflection in

the mirror on the closet door. He looked like he could be her father with that beard. Which was kind of icky, considering he was snuggled up against her on his bed and twirling one of her ringlets around his finger. One of her out-of-control ringlets. Anabelle pulled a couple curls to the front, then pushed them to the side. No matter what she did, she looked like Little Orphan Annie. Only, with sawdust-colored hair. And black clothes instead of red. She still hadn't changed out of her orchestra uniform.

Matt nuzzled his nose into Anabelle's neck. "Well, do you like it?" he asked, popping open the top of the box. The inside was lined with mauve velvet and smelled of overripe berries.

Anabelle forced a grateful smile. "I love it."

"Yeah?"

"Yeah."

"Good, 'cause I stayed up till four working on it. The eyes were a killer."

The miniature version of Matt's big brown eyes gazed up at Anabelle with a pleading puppy-dog expression that seemed to say, *Please don't leave me. Never, ever leave me.* In his tiny clay hands he held a tiny bouquet of clay dandelions, just like the ones the real Matt had used to woo her—that day on his porch when he'd told Anabelle she was "friendly" and later admitted that was code for "cute." She still had the wilted weeds pressed in a dictionary under her bed.

Anabelle's stomach was folding in on itself, like tightly creased origami. The berry smell. It was drowning her senses. She shut the jewelry box, and as the clasp clicked into place, she imagined having this thing in her dorm room next year. She pictured people spotting it on her dresser. Any boy who walked in would get the message loud and clear: This girl is taken.

"You don't seem too psyched," Matt said, sitting up rigidly.

"No, I am," Anabelle said. "I'm just trying to figure out what to put in it. I don't really wear jewelry." Didn't he know that after dating her for a year?

"But I thought maybe you could start. Since you'll be a college girl now."

"Yeah, maybe." Anabelle pushed aside Matt's cigarette packs and put the jewelry box on his nightstand, out of her sight.

"Or you could use it to store the poems I've written you."

"Some of them," she said. "They won't all fit."

A burst of singing came from downstairs. Ugh, weren't the Players sick of *Cabaret* by now? Anabelle was. And she hadn't even been singing those songs the last few months, just accompanying them. Sure, she got that it was their cast party and all. *But c'mon,* she thought, *get over yourselves.*

Matt cracked each of his big toes. "You don't like it."

"No, I do. I said I did."

"Only because I asked."

"Matt, it's amazing," Anabelle assured him. "It's just . . . so much." She leaned in and planted a kiss on his cheek, careful to avoid the side of his beard.

He jerked his face back, his eyes narrowing. "Why didn't you kiss me on the lips?" he asked.

"It's just, I don't like the feeling of hair on my mouth," Anabelle told him. "It's scratchy." Downstairs, one of the Players' voices rose above the rest. It was Lexi, Matt's sister—always the star of the show whether onstage or off.

"You're my girlfriend. You should like kissing me no matter what."

Anabelle sighed and clunked the back of her head against the headboard. She did it again, this time hard enough that it would leave a little bruise—a tender spot that she knew would be sore when she touched it later. Matt didn't seem to notice; he didn't even look at her.

Anabelle stared up at the track lighting. One of the bulbs flashed out.

"Wow," Matt said, with that forced-air laugh he gave when he was nervous. "You actually look like you want to hit me."

"No," Anabelle answered. But now that he pointed it out, she realized she kind of did want to.

"Go ahead." He rolled up his T-shirt and offered her his arm.

"I'm not going to hit you."

"Do it."

Reluctantly, she made a fist and punched him, her knuckles thudding against his skin.

"What was that?" he asked. "The wind blowing? I barely felt a thing."

The Players hit the crescendo at the end of the song. Anabelle could just picture them, shooting each other satisfied smiles as if they'd invented harmony.

She geared up again, squeezing her hand into a ball of momentum, then took aim, zeroing in on a spot halfway between Matt's shoulder and elbow. Her swing landed with a smack.

"Aw," Matt screamed, "you didn't have to do it *that* hard. Jesus!"

He had a crazy look in his eyes, as if he were going to hit her back.

Anabelle's head fizzed like a just-opened soda can. She wasn't sure if it was because it felt good to hurt him or because she was afraid of what he might do. Leaping off the bed, she bolted for the door. "I need to be away from you right now," she said, hearing her voice tremble. "And don't even think about following me."

"Fine!" he yelled after her as she sprinted for the stairs. "If that's how you want to be when we only have three months left in the same town!" But she kept running—past the kitchen, where the most notoriously out-of-tune Player was whining about her love life to Matt's mom. And past the living room, where Lexi was standing on the coffee table leading the rest of the group in a rendition of *Cabaret*'s "Telephone Song." Normally, this song would've made Anabelle laugh because down in the pit, Tobin Wood, the cellist, always lip-synched along when the Players attempted German accents. But Tobin wasn't here now—he never came to cast parties—and the accents only grated on her.

Anabelle hoped Lexi didn't notice her running past. Or, well, maybe part of her hoped that she did. That Lexi would ditch the party to comfort her. After all, Lexi was always telling Anabelle that she was her best friend. And isn't that what best friends did? Put helping each other over everything else?

By the time Anabelle got to the basement, she realized her hand was still all balled up. She spread her fingers, revealing four crescent-moon indentations along the bottom of her palm where her nails had been digging in.

♪✱

The little upright piano looked out of place amid the sprawling wires, amps, and electric guitars. Matt was in something like four bands, but they rarely rehearsed. That was fine with Anabelle; it meant she could practice here, too.

She settled into the cushiony bench and positioned her hands on the keys, ready to drown out the singing upstairs. She had just figured out by ear a solo version of "'Round Midnight," and as she played it she tried to hit the notes exactly like Thelonious Monk did in the recording. She savored each chord, the strange harmonies dissolving together like ice cubes in hot coffee. This piano had the most amazing sound: it was woody and warm and reminded her of what it felt like to have all her clothes smell like campfire. She didn't even mind that it was a little out of tune; the subtle warble gave it an old-timey feel. And that key with no top, the second-to-lowest C, helped her navigate the bottom register of the keyboard. The exposed rectangle of wood stood out like a missing tooth.

Playing this piece, she didn't have to think about Matt telling her what was wrong with her, telling her that she didn't hang out with his friends enough, or that when she did hang out with them, she was too quiet and kept him from being the outgoing guy he wanted to be. She didn't have to think about how to convince him that if he would just chill out, things would be fine next year, that they could totally handle a long-distance relationship. Right now, all that existed were trickling whole-tone scales, rhythmic bass notes, beats of silence that made her want to hold her breath—and, of course, if her interpretation was to sound authentically Monk, dissonant intervals.

When she hammered into those just right, she swore she could feel the backs of her eyeballs vibrate.

♪＊

She'd gone through the piece probably nine times—no, maybe more like eleven or twelve?—when someone slid in beside her on the bench. Her hands slammed down on the keys, making a strange chord that could've easily fit in in a Monk tune.

She figured it was Matt coming to make up. But when she turned she saw that the bearded guy beside her was a rusty redhead, not a brunette. Actually, he wasn't all that bearded either. Just pleasantly scruffy.

"You bop when you play," Jonah said, smiling the crooked half smile that always made Anabelle's ears warm.

She shrugged and pressed her foot nervously up and down on the sustain pedal.

"Keep playing," he said. "I liked it."

"Well, I can't with you sitting right here," she told him, tapping the pedal faster.

Jonah was on the lighting crew for the show and, like Anabelle, he was decked out in all black. The fabric of his faded black jeans butted up against the baggy dress pants she'd borrowed from her mom. Anabelle knew she should probably scoot away from him. She took her foot off the pedal but for some dumb reason kept her leg where it was.

"You okay?" Jonah asked.

"Yeah, what do you mean?" *You should really move*, Anabelle told herself. If Matt came down here and saw them, he'd freak.

"Matt's sulking in his room," Jonah said. "Smoking weed by himself."

"Aren't there, like, a ton of girls up there for you to hit

on?" she asked, pointing at the ceiling. The sing-along seemed to have stopped and was replaced by a general party din peppered with occasional shrieks of laughter.

Jonah shoved her teasingly. "You think I'm way more of a player than I actually am," he said. "I mean, I'm definitely not a *Player*. But I'm also not a player."

"Riiiight."

"Seriously. I'd way rather be hanging out down here with a girl who's totally taken than a bunch of semidrunk girls in fishnets and leather."

"You like the costumes, admit it."

"Well, yeah, they do look good on some people. But their makeup is way overdone."

Anabelle knew exactly which girls Jonah would think looked good in those getups. They were the same ones he gave his trying-not-to-look-like-I'm-staring stare when they wore low-cut tops and tight jeans. Stuff she could never pull off.

Jonah gently hit a high B-flat with his pinkie, then started walking his fingers down the keyboard in half steps. "I can talk to him if you want," he said.

She knew by his somber tone that he meant Matt. But she pretended she didn't. "Talk to who?"

"Your boyfriend," he answered in a tone that said, *Don't play dumb.*

But still, she did. "About what?" she asked as innocently as possible.

His thumb hit middle C. "Tell him he's being a dick."

The thought of Jonah defending her was kind of exciting. But she knew it would only cause trouble. "What do you mean?"

He gave her an "Oh, please" look.

"I mean, yeah, things are a little weird," she conceded. "But I can handle it."

Jonah's fingers crept into the lower register. He leaned over her lap, playing every note until he reached the missing-tooth key. When he hit that one, he looked up at her and raised an eyebrow. Did that mean something? *No,* she told herself. *Of course it didn't.* And even if it did, it wouldn't matter. She was with Matt. She would be with Matt forever.

Still, she couldn't help feeling let down when Jonah took his hand off the piano and sat back up.

"I've gotta ask you something," he said. "Something personal."

"Yeah, okay." Anabelle had this uncomfortable sense

anabelle seulliere

that he was about to ask her something that would throw her relationship with Matt into turmoil.

"Matt's my best friend and all," he said, "but I keep wondering . . ."

Oh God, was he hitting on her?

". . . why do you stay with him? Why don't you just dump him? I mean, you're leaving. Going far, far away. And there'll be plenty of cool guys at Oberlin, I'm sure."

Not a come-on. Anabelle was surprised by how disappointed she was that the question hadn't been something like "Why wasn't it you and me instead?" or "Haven't you always felt like there was something between us?" She'd heard stories about seniors confessing their secret love for each other at the end of the year and she couldn't help but wonder if that might happen with her and Jonah.

"Sorry," Jonah said. "It's none of my business."

"No, no," she said. "I get what you're saying. But I don't know. It's like this. Matt's the first boy who ever wanted to date me. And I can't imagine being with anyone else. Or, at least, I can't picture another guy falling for me like he did."

"If you were single, the guys would flock," Jonah said. "They'd be all over you."

Wait, did he mean *he* would? Anabelle wanted to find

out. She wanted to be able to get herself to return that longing—was it longing?—look he was giving her. She wanted the awkward silence to continue. But instead she started talking a mile a minute, not really sure what was going to come out. "I fell in love with Matt," she blathered, "because he seemed like the saddest person in the world. He wrote me a poem. And he drew a face on the bottom. It was like this egg head with a frown. And somehow that piece of paper, with the drawing and the poem, it was pure sorrow. I've never seen anyone our age capture sadness so perfectly. For some reason, that was irresistible to me. I guess it still is."

Jonah got an amused smile on his face that just grew and grew.

"What's that look for?" Man, why did she just tell him all of that?

"No, it's just, I never pegged you as a sucker for a sad sack. You seem so happy-go-lucky."

Anabelle wasn't sure if she should take that as a compliment or an insult. "Happy-go-lucky" made her think of a girl in pigtails licking a giant lollipop, running around with a duck-shaped floatie around her waist.

"Hey," he said, nudging her leg with his.

"What?"

His irises glowed yellowish like that tiger's-eye stone she had when she was a kid. "Stay out of my dreams," he said, suddenly serious.

"Stay out of what?"

"My dreams."

Maybe this really was going in *that* direction. "You dreamed about me?"

"You're quick."

"What'd you dream?"

"If you think I'm telling you, you're out of your mind."

"Okay, I'm out of my mind."

"I never should've brought it up." Now *his* foot was tapping the sustain pedal. The piano shook slightly every time he pressed down on it.

"But you did," she said, wiping her sweaty palms on her pants. "You must want to tell me."

"Trust me, I don't."

"If you're trying to make me beg, I'm not gonna."

"Good. I don't want you to."

Anabelle felt her heart rate rising as Jonah increased the speed of his foot tapping. She grabbed his knee. "You're driving me crazy," she told him.

His foot froze.

"Please tell me," she said, her hand still clutching his knee.

"No," he insisted.

"Why not?"

"Because," he said. "It was disturbing."

Anabelle didn't get to hear exactly what was so disturbing because just as she was about to ask, there were footsteps running down the basement stairs. Footsteps too light to be Matt's. Still, she jumped up off the piano bench, trying to breathe deeply to stop the redness that she was sure was rushing to her face.

And then there was humming—a girl's voice humming "Don't Tell Mama," another hit from *Cabaret*. Thank God, it was just Lexi. She pranced into the basement doing her dance routine, her high blond ponytail bouncing with each fishnet-legged kick. When she saw Anabelle and Jonah, she halted, her arm midair. "Um, am I, like, interrupting something?" she asked.

"No, of course not," Anabelle said, rushing up to Lexi. "I was actually just about to come find you. I haven't seen you all night!" She plopped down on the threadbare carpeted steps and pulled Lexi into the spot next to her.

"Where's my brother?" Lexi asked, still looking suspicious. Her vinyl bustier creaked with every movement.

"In his room," Jonah answered quickly, swinging around on the piano bench to face them. "Probably passed out by now."

"Good," Lexi said. "I'm not in the mood for his mopeyness right now. It's enough to have to deal with the play being over. It's like giving up your baby for adoption. Only worse, because there's no chance you'll ever get to see it again. Plus, I can't believe how many seniors there are. Way more than last year. We're losing like half our actors."

"Funny," Jonah said, "Anabelle and I were just talking about how *she's* leaving us, too."

"Don't remind me," Lexi said, sinking her chin into her hands.

He smirked. "I was just telling her how she's gonna be a dude magnet."

Lexi tightened her ponytail. "Oh, totally," she said. "But how disappointed will they be when they find out she's basically married?"

"We had actually moved past that onto another topic," Anabelle jumped in, not liking where they were going. "Jonah had a dream about me. He says it's disturbing."

Lexi slapped her knees excitedly. "Yeah? What happened in it?"

Jonah shot Anabelle a you-are-going-to-regret-this look. "Nothing," he snapped.

"*Something* must've happened if it was so disturbing," Lexi said. "What'd she do? Try to kill you? Bore you to death with jazz theory?"

"Shut up," Anabelle said. "If I were going to kill him, I'd do something more effective. Drop a piano on his head maybe."

"Is that what she did, Jonah?" Lexi teased. "Or was it more of an S-and-M type of thing? C'mon, you know Anabelle would make a hot dominatrix."

This was Lexi's latest obsession. Trying to convince Anabelle she should be more of a bad girl. Last week she'd talked Anabelle into trying on her *Cabaret* costume. Anabelle had stood around in it for five never-ending minutes while Lexi giggled—gleefully? mockingly?—and then finally agreed to undo all the little hook-and-eye closures in the back. Very, very slowly.

"She was dripping hot wax on your nipples, wasn't she?" Lexi prodded.

Jonah glared at her, exhaling loudly through his nostrils.

Lexi shot up. "Well, sorry it had come to this, but you've

really left us no choice," she said in that singsong tone she used when she was about to do something that was fun for her but not for the person she was about to do it to.

Anabelle knew what was coming. It was a well-known fact that Jonah was crazy ticklish. Really, you just had to wiggle your fingers by his neck to get him going.

Lexi charged Jonah and dug into his stomach. "Help me!" she called to Anabelle as Jonah thrashed around.

Anabelle reluctantly got up and joined in. She tickled Jonah along his ribs, his sides, his gut. She realized she'd never touched another grown guy in these places aside from Matt. Jonah felt different—stronger and more squishy all at the same time. Under his armpit was really warm. A little damp. When she tickled him there, he dropped to the floor, laughing uncontrollably. It was the kind of laugh that sounded like it hurt.

He rolled around, struggling, then forcefully grabbed hold of Anabelle's wrists. "Stop!" he screamed, his face red and tear-streaked. "Seriously, stop!"

Anabelle choked on her breath. Lexi jumped back and let go of him as if he were a pot of boiling water she'd just grabbed without oven mitts.

Jonah stood up, lifting Anabelle by her wrists, and

slammed her against the wall. "You want to know what it was about?"

She nodded, not sure if she really did anymore.

"Jesus, Jonah, let go of her," Lexi said. "We were just messing with you."

Jonah loosened his grip. But he leaned down and put his nose right up against Anabelle's. "I dreamed I was lying in my bed," he said. "On my back. And you came flying into my room. Gliding through the air. And you stopped right above me. Just hung there, floating." His breath was hot on her upper lip. "And then you kissed me. And kissed me and kissed me. And it just wouldn't stop."

"Wow," Lexi said. "That *is* disturbing."

♪✳

That night, as Anabelle lay awake in her bed, she felt as if her insides might erupt right out of her skin like molten lava. She wanted to scream; she wanted to break something.

But she had to keep quiet. Her little twin sisters were asleep in the bunk bed on the other side of the room.

She got up, thinking maybe she'd call Matt. She'd left his house without saying goodbye. The plan had been for her to sleep over, like she did most Saturday nights, but somehow tonight she felt like she'd rather be woken up by her sisters at dawn than get to sleep in in Lexi's room. Plus, she had thought the walk home would clear her head. It didn't.

She crept downstairs, knowing exactly where to place her foot on each step to avoid creaking. In the kitchen she picked up the phone. She started to dial, then hung up. Matt would probably be unintelligible by now and talking to him would just make her feel worse.

She went to the bathroom, flipped on the light, and sat on the cold tiles, wishing she could make the queasiness in her stomach go away. *Maybe you can,* she thought. She raised the toilet seat and leaned over the bowl, sticking her finger down her throat. This was how you did it, right? She'd seen kids at parties make themselves throw up this way when they'd had too much to drink.

Nothing would come out, though, no matter how hard she strained. All it did was gag her.

She stood up and looked in the mirror. Her skin was all gray. Tiny purple blood vessels circled her eyes. She stared at her zombie-esque face for a minute or two, then went digging through her mother's makeup bag looking for some concealer. Just in case she wasn't herself by morning.

{ A **MIX TAPE** *for the* **BEARS** }

tobin wood

When Tobin pulled his dad's WoodWorks Plumbing van onto the Fletchers' car-packed lawn, he saw something truly horrible in his headlights: the profile of a girl sitting on the trampoline, banging her brains out with her fist. The worst part about it was, it was Anabelle Seulliere, the only reason he'd come to Matt's graduation party to begin with. Each time she pounded her head, her corkscrew curls shook violently—those curls that were a girl version of his. Those curls that made him wonder during concerts if people noticed they looked alike and thought they belonged together.

You've gotta do something, Tobin thought. But what? Maybe she didn't want to see anyone right now. And shouldn't the person comforting her be her spoiled brat of a boyfriend? Or was he the one who'd made her this upset?

Tobin was having trouble thinking because of the racket coming from the house. Sounded like some band was "rocking out," as wannabe musicians called it. All he could hear was a blast of unsteady bass and drums. *How is it possible to rock out,* he wondered, *if you can't keep a beat?*

Suddenly Anabelle started hitting herself with both fists at the same time. She was doing it so hard, Tobin was afraid she might crack her skull.

He slammed on the gas, heading across the lawn toward the trampoline. Anabelle squinted into the headlights, then dove down into the net as if hiding from him. *Great,* he thought. *Am I supposed to pretend I didn't see her?* But there was no turning back now. He'd probably have to circle around the trampoline just to turn back, anyway; despite all of his dad's training, Tobin still wasn't any good at reversing in the van with no rearview mirror.

He stopped alongside the trampoline and rolled down his window. Anabelle was sprawled out, facedown. She didn't sit up. Maybe it *wasn't* too late to sneak off unnoticed. No, he couldn't do that. What if she was really in trouble? But what if she didn't want him to be the one to help her? *Jesus, stop being such a wimp,* he told himself. *Just talk to her.*

"Anabelle?" he said finally.

No answer. Maybe he didn't say it loudly enough for her to hear him over the rock stars? Or maybe she wanted him to leave. Yeah, probably.

Just as he was about to drive away, he heard a faint *Mm-hmm* and *Is that you, Tobin?*

"Yeah, it's me," he said, thrilled that she recognized his voice.

"Did you, um, see me just now?" It was a little hard to make out what she was saying—she seemed to have her face pressed into the trampoline net. Tobin wondered if he could just pretend he hadn't heard her and let the question go.

But she asked again: "Did you see all those mosquitoes flying around my head? I was swatting and swatting at them."

He had this feeling that she knew that he knew she was lying. It was too early for mosquito season. And those punches she was giving herself were not little bug-killing smacks. But he went along with it anyway, relieved she'd cleared the air with an excuse. "They're gone now?" he asked. "The mosquitoes, I mean." Duh, what else would he mean?

"Yeah, they're gone."

"Um, do you want me to go away?" he asked. "I mean, you can be alone if you want. I just, y'know, you asked me to come to the party." He looked over at the house. Through the living-room windows he could see college pennants hanging from the ceiling in a row of colorful pointy triangles. Matt's little sister was standing on the couch directing a game or something—she always seemed to figure out how to be in charge even when it wasn't her party. Kids mingled around her in pre-hookup mode, the room dotted with red plastic beer cups. In a smaller window below that one he saw Matt Fletcher's bearded face bouncing around, a guitar in his hands. So that's where he was. "There isn't really anyone else in there I want to see," he told Anabelle. "But I don't mind if you don't want me to—"

"No, stay," she said, cutting him off. "I don't want to see anyone in there either." Wow, did that mean she and Matt were fighting? Did that mean he had a shot with her?

Who was he kidding? She'd never split up with Matt.

The drums gave one last shimmery bash and then,

thank God, the so-called music was over. Matt's head disappeared from the basement window and Tobin hoped he
wasn't coming outside.

Tobin shut off his headlights but stayed in the still-
running van, pushing his thumbs through holes in the
sleeves of his hoodie and drumming them against the
steering wheel. A chorus of crickets chirped all around
him. If he listened carefully he could hear one that stood
out—offbeat but still part of the group somehow. The solo-
ist in the choir.

"So are you gonna join me or what?" Anabelle asked.
She sounded annoyed.

"Oh. Right, yeah, of course." God, why was he so retarded
when it came to girls? Or, girl, really. Anabelle was the only
one who turned him into such an idiot. "I was, uh, just getting something." He reached into the glove compartment
and pulled out a tape labeled FOR ANNABELLE.

Tobin loved the rattly feeling of a cassette tape in his
hands. Cassettes were old-school and romantic. You could
record onto them and practice from them and play them in
your parents' beat-up cars. And he knew that Anabelle felt
the same way. It was the first thing they'd ever bonded over.

Before this moment, here's how Tobin had imagined

the handoff of the FOR ANNABELLE tape going down: He'd be saying goodbye to her after having not talked to her enough at the party. Then he'd pull the tape out of his pocket, push it into her hands, and kind of run away like the nervous freak that he was. Never in a million years did he think he'd be able to share this tape with her, live and in-person—to actually see her reaction to it.

Okay, here goes, Tobin thought. His hand quivered slightly as he popped the cassette into the stereo and pressed play.

He got out of the van and hoisted himself onto the trampoline, then sat a safe distance from Anabelle, who still hadn't budged from her uncomfortable-looking face-down position. *Should you have sat closer to her?* he wondered as the hiss of the recording kicked in. *Just, like, a foot closer?* And then in came the piano, beginning with four bars of sparse chords. Next, the cello with its soft sweeping melody. Tobin imagined that this was *him* on cello, with Anabelle on piano, and that he was looking deep into her pale green sea-glass eyes, following her slow and steady tempo. He wondered if she was picturing playing the piece with him, too.

You definitely should've sat closer to her, he thought. But it would probably seem strange to do that at this point. Too obvious and predatory. Maybe he could offer her his hoodie? It was still a little too cold to be outside in just a T-shirt and her arms were covered in goose bumps.

"This is nice," Anabelle said when the violin came in, joining the piano and cello. "What is it?"

"Oh, the music?" Tobin said, as if he didn't even realize it was on—as if it had just randomly started playing in his car. "Schubert's Piano Trio in B-flat. The slow movement." He was glad she liked it but decided he'd wait till later to tell her the tape was for her, that it was, in fact, an entire mix of pieces they could play together. Maybe. Someday. If she wanted to.

"It's so sad," she said.

"But in a good way, right?" He hoped she wasn't changing her mind about liking it.

"No, in a totally good way." For the first time, she turned to look at him. Her forehead and nose were imprinted with the grid of the net. "You know what it makes me feel like?"

"What?"

"Lie down like me," she told him. "With your face in the trampoline."

He did. And in the process got a little closer to her—still

leaving just enough space so that they weren't touching. He hoped she wouldn't freak out and think he was coming on to her. But she was the one who'd said to lie down, so he figured he wasn't breaking any boundaries.

"See all that grass down there?" she asked.

Hovering over the lawn, all he could see was grass. "Yeah, I see it," he said. His voice cracked a little because he was thinking about moving his sneaker over to touch hers, which, of course, he didn't.

"So this music," she said, "it makes me feel like, even though I'm looking at a whole bunch of grass, all I can see is a single blade."

This was what was great about Anabelle. She spoke so poetically about music. Tobin knew what he liked and what he didn't like, but talking about it never came naturally to him. "That is the absolute most perfect way to describe it," he told her.

"You're just saying that," she said. "You don't even know what I mean."

"No, I do. I know exactly what you mean."

"Prove it."

"That single blade you're looking at?" he said. "I'm looking at the same one."

"Yeah?" She giggled. "Which one?"

"That one right . . . there." As he pointed, his finger brushed her cheek. He quickly withdrew his hand, but she didn't even seem to notice he'd touched her.

"You mean the one farthest to the right in the clump under my nose?" she asked with the delight of a four-year-old.

"Yes," he said. "That's the one!"

He was suddenly overcome with the desire to kiss her. Out here in the dark, no one would ever know. *What is wrong with you?* he asked himself. *She's got a boyfriend.*

"Tobin?" Anabelle said as the dainty last notes of the trio faded and the spooky chords of the next piece started up. It was Beethoven's Sonata for Piano and Cello no. 2 in G Minor. He couldn't wait to hear how she'd describe this one.

"Yeah?" He glanced up to see if she'd moved her face out of the net. She hadn't, so he put his back down, too. He kind of liked this position. He felt like a superhero. Well, one who could only fly three feet above the ground. But still.

"You seem like you can keep a secret."

Yes! She saw him as trustworthy. "Sure, I can do that," he said. "Who would I tell, anyway?"

"I'm kinda having this problem," she confessed. She was tapping one of her fingers on the net in time with the music. She must've picked up on the gorgeous way the rhythm had just changed.

"What is it?"

"Well, it's embarrassing. And it makes me feel like a horrible person."

"No, there's nothing that could possibly be horrible about you, Anabelle," he said. "We all have our downsides. But that just means you're human." He still wasn't touching her. Not physically. But he felt as if their minds were melding in a way that was completely tangible.

"So . . . I think I like someone," she said slowly. "Someone other than Matt."

"Really?" It was *him*. No it wasn't. Could it be? Definitely not. Or maybe it could. Who else would it be? Just then, the piano and cello struck a triumphant major chord. *That must be a sign*, he thought. *It's me.*

"Yeah," she said. "The thing is, I'm not sure if he likes me back. I mean, it's hard to tell—but I'm pretty sure he does."

It *had* to be him. God, he was so stupid! He should've been giving her more clues all along that he liked her—no, loved her. Liking a girl is what you did in second grade; this was much bigger.

"The thing is," she said, "I don't feel right about trying

to find out where this other thing could go unless I break up with Matt first. But I don't know, it's kind of hard for me to imagine anyone *but* Matt being interested in me. So maybe it's not worth it."

Should he just come out and say he was absolutely, positively, without a doubt, interested?

Should he grab her and kiss her?

No. He would not be a typical guy. He would not be one of those guys who just saw women as objects. He'd handle this respectfully. Like a gentleman.

"I'm sure he'd be into you if you broke up with Matt," Tobin said.

"You think?" she asked, turning on her side to face him.

He rolled over to face her, too. She was giving him this funny little smile. *Coy* was the word for that type of smile.

Okay, he thought. *That's it. No more waiting around.* This was going to be his best shot with her and she was making it clear that she wanted him. If he waited any longer, she might decide to go back to Matt. This was perfect, actually. They could have a summer romance. Ride bikes, picnics, hikes up the bluffs. And when it came time to part ways in the fall, well, that would suck. But at least she would've been his first girlfriend.

The piano was arpeggiating up and down as if to say,

Time is running out—go for it! He closed his eyes and took a deep breath like he always did before cannonballing off the bluffs into the ocean, then leaned in to where he assumed her lips would be and—

—and her lips weren't there. He got the side of her ear. He opened his eyes to see that she'd turned her head. She had this look on her face as if she'd just seen the climax of a horror flick.

Tobin sat straight up, his thumbs shooting through the holes in his hoodie. "What—what happened?" he asked. "I thought—"

"I'm so sorry," she said, hugging her knees. "I didn't mean—"

"I've never tried that with anyone before."

"Oh no, don't tell me that. Now I feel awful."

"So do I," he said. "I don't get it. It seemed like you wanted me to."

"No, I guess I wasn't being clear," she said. "I was talking about someone else."

"Who?"

"It doesn't matter."

"It does to me."

She was rocking back and forth, making the trampoline shift underneath him. "You have to promise not to tell anyone."

"I won't. Just tell me. You owe me that after all this."

"It's Jonah," she said.

Wait, what? *Jonah?* Jonah Wilder? Jonah Wilder who would flirt with anything with boobs? Who could get any girl he wanted? Who probably slept with more girls than any other guy in the history of Normal High?

"You're being quiet," Anabelle said.

"Yeah." Tobin's skin was burning up. The music had just gotten to the syrupy part that always reminded him of scenes in cheesy old movies, when a couple has their first kiss. "I've gotta go," he said. He stood up and bounced a couple times on the trampoline, sweat trickling down the insides of his arms.

"Wait," she said. "Stay a little longer? This feels so abrupt. Shouldn't we talk things through some more?"

"I don't have anything else to say." Tobin turned and jumped down to the grass. "Here," he said, after he got in the van. "If you're gonna stay out here, you'll need this." He took off his hoodie and tossed it at her through the window. He'd thrown it harder than he meant to and he thought he heard the zipper hit her face. Nice impression to leave her with the last time he saw her, probably ever. Unless they ran into each other coming and going from their jobs on the boardwalk. Which he hoped they wouldn't.

As he drove off he watched her in the sideview mirror getting smaller and smaller, clutching his red sweatshirt like a security blanket.

♪※

Back at home, Tobin stormed straight to his room and pulled out his cello. Instinctively, he started playing his part in Schubert's Piano Trio. He'd been practicing it a lot lately so that he'd be ready to try it with Anabelle once she got the tape. Well, that wasn't going to happen anymore. No, he needed to go solo from now on. He dug around in his music folder until he found the Prelude to Bach's Suite no. 1 in G Major, just meant for a single cello. He opened the photocopied pages and placed them on his music stand. There, that was more like it. This piece was made for him, and him only.

Tobin's bow glided over the strings, lightly hitting the first arpeggios. As the piece built, he slowly started throwing more weight into his arm and pressing his callused fingers into the fret board more forcefully. The gritty low notes were his favorites—they made him feel like his veins were wires on a circuit board and his blood was electricity.

Just as he was about to hit the final chord, a noise came through the wall from his dad's bedroom. It was a sound Tobin had grown used to, but somehow it never became less unpleasant. And it was different almost every time; his dad rarely brought home the same woman twice, or at least not twice in a row. The one he had in there right now kept saying "Steve, Steve, Steeeve" and panting as if she'd just finished a triathlon. There was some banging, too.

He had to get out of here. Now.

He laid his cello on his bed without packing it in its case and ran back to the van.

♪❋

Tobin zoomed down Oceanside Drive and circled around WhirrrlyWorld, with its swirling lights and gleeful screams of terror. He pulled into the parking lot, figuring this night would end the way most nights ended when he couldn't deal with his dad's bedroom antics: riding the Ferris wheel alone over and over until the park closed. But as he drove around looking for a spot, the cotton-candy-funnel-cake smell made his stomach feel as if he'd been riding the ferry on choppy waters and he decided to go somewhere else.

But where?

He sped off, the wind slapping his face. A car horn blared at him and he realized he'd just run a red. "Stupid traffic light," he grumbled. Up until a few days ago, it had only been a stop sign. The traffic light was one of those new "safety features" requested by the people who'd built those enormous beach houses that looked as if they could eat all the other Normal houses for lunch. Normal had never had a traffic light before and, as far as Tobin knew, nobody had died because of it. So why did they need one now?

Before he could get over his traffic-light frustration, the van lurched over a giant speed bump—another fun new safety feature.

Tobin started to worry that he might get in an accident, so he pulled into the next driveway, marked by a mailbox with an elaborately painted name, SINGLETARY. The driveway was long and gravelly and led to a mega-cottage—a crazy castley-looking place with towers and turrets, where he'd helped his dad install a pool last summer. He was pretty sure he was safe hanging out here while he collected himself; there were no other cars in the driveway. And vacation season didn't start for a couple more weeks. As he parked behind some towering bushes, he realized he'd never turned off the music in his car. Now it was spewing Brahms. Just for piano and cello.

The Anabelle tape. The goddamn Anabelle tape.

He couldn't believe how stupid he'd been for making it. For thinking she might secretly like him back.

Tobin slammed on the eject button and the cassette shot out of the stereo. He grabbed it and yanked at the thin brown ribbon. He kept pulling and pulling until none of the tape was left in the plastic shell, until it was a mangled heap in his lap. "Fucking hell!" he yelled as he got out of the van and tossed the whole mess into the bushes.

What were these ridiculously high bushes doing here anyway? Tobin didn't remember them from when he'd worked on the pool. That weird pool that was supposed to look like a pond or a marsh or something, where his dad kept making lewd comments about the supercurvy girl who lived here. She was about Tobin's age and had some hyphenated name like Mary-something and she kept trying to talk to him while he was working. He was never interested in her, though; his dad didn't get why. He'd always shake his head in dismay and say something like, "You should really get a piece of that."

Ugh, his dad was disgusting! As if girls were made of pieces! What piece did he think Tobin should go for anyway? Was there a certain piece his dad was after when he hit on ladies at bars and the beach? And had he loved *all* the pieces of Tobin's mom before she died? Or was it none of them? Because that's sure what it seemed like, with the parade of women he brought into the bed he used to share with his *wife*.

Tobin picked up a handful of driveway pebbles and started tossing them at the lawn one by one.

What was wrong with this town? Why was it that in Normal, most single women went for a sleaze like his dad and the Anabelles of the world went for the Jonahs? It didn't make any sense. He couldn't wait to get out of here, to get away from these people, to get his scholarship and go to the conservatory.

He threw the rocks harder and harder, now aiming them at the gutter pipes along the side of the house. They made a satisfying *plink* each time they hit.

Tobin wondered if this was how things worked everywhere. He couldn't really imagine being as crazy about any girl as he was for Anabelle. But even if he met someone just as incredible as her, he didn't think he had what it would take to win a girl over. He would never be a Jonah. Did that mean he'd never have a girlfriend?

He leaned over and picked up the biggest rock he could find—about the size of a harmonica—and, without really thinking, hurled it into a large bay window on the second floor. The glass shattered, leaving a jagged hole in one of the panes.

Tobin couldn't believe what he'd just done. He knew he should feel awful, but for some reason he felt a surge of power. Like he could lift a tree out of the ground if he wanted to. And he could wield that tree like a baseball bat, demolishing this entire house—knocking all three stories into the sea.

Tobin stretched his arms out to his sides, feeling the adrenaline race to his fingertips. He started running around the bushes, angling his body to the left then the right, as if he were a little boy imitating a plane. Then, with a running jump, he did a cartwheel—or his best approximation of one—and then a somersault. He did three of those in a row before tumbling onto his back, out of breath. He inhaled the salty ocean breeze wafting from the shore and looked up at the bushes, black against the dark denim sky. There was something menacing about the shape of them, but he couldn't place it exactly, until he realized they were cut to look like a couple of bears. One was on its hind legs and the other on all fours. Out there, with no people around, the bears seemed almost real to Tobin, as if they might pounce on him at any second.

"Bring it!" he yelled up at them. "I'm all yours!"

{ **BURNT** *Popcorn* }

jonah wilder

By the time Jonah's mom sent him to the health-food store for pumpkin seeds and cascara pills, he had already spent all day peeling the waxy skins off of her fruits and vegetables and making her countless pots of clove-infused tea. She would've taken care of the tea herself, she'd told him, but she was too busy washing her hands to death and making sure her finger and toenails were clipped down to the flesh. These were all necessary steps toward ridding

herself of the parasite in her intestines. It had been growing there for three days now. Or so she said.

Jonah's mom always thought she had something. In
fact, it was the antibiotics the doctor had prescribed for
her recent "bladder infection" that she blamed for this
worm, or whatever it *really* was that was, uh, giving her
bathroom troubles. Not that he even wanted to think
about that. Still, he went on his assignment to find her
natural laxatives.

He got to the store just as they were closing and flashed
the cute cashier an apologetic smile—a smile with just
the right side of his mouth, which he knew made pretty
much all girls swoon. "Take your time," the cashier said,
the air from the ceiling fan ruffling her thin bangs. He
thought he remembered her from school a few years
back—maybe she was a senior when he was a freshman?
Lately he'd been finding himself really attracted to older
girls, especially ones like this cashier, who could pull off
little-girl braids and still look sophisticated. As she rang
him up she kept giving him flirtatious glances and he
considered asking her if she wanted to take a walk on
the beach when she got off work. *No*, he told himself. *Stay
out of trouble.* These things never ended well. Or not simply,
at least.

He decided he'd stop by Matt's on his way home. His mom could wait for her pumpkin seeds and cascara pills. And if she checked herself in to the hospital again just to be told there was nothing wrong with her, that was fine with him.

♪❋

The Fletchers' back door was unlocked, as usual. Jonah let himself in and called out for Matt. No answer. Just as he started running upstairs to check Matt's room, Jeanie came into the hallway. She was wearing a silky red kimono, unbelted, over shorts and a tank top.

"Matty's not here," she said, waving a pot holder in the air as if flagging him down. "It's just me."

"Hey, Jeanie," he said, breathing through his mouth to keep from inhaling a burnt-food smell. "You cooking or something?"

"Well, sorta," she said. There was a crazy noise coming from the kitchen. A whole bunch of rumbling. And something like pops from a cap gun.

Jonah couldn't remember ever having seen Jeanie cook a meal. She was more of an order-in kind of woman.

"Sorry, I actually have to get back in there," she said, hurrying into the kitchen. "You can join me if you want."

Jonah followed her to the stove. The noises had died down. But the smell was way worse.

Jeanie uncovered the pot and peered inside. "Shit, shit, shit!" she said. Jonah watched her under the dim range light tasting a piece of popcorn. She had her hair up, but there wasn't really enough to form a ponytail, so it was falling out all over the sides in black wisps. Jeanie was the master of little-girl sophistication. She had it down better, even, than the health-food-store cashier. Way better.

Jeanie swallowed the kernel and wrinkled her nose, groaning. She sank her fingers into her hair, pushing her fingertips against her scalp.

Jonah wasn't really sure what to say to her, or why he was sticking around without Matt there. *Just make some small talk,* he told himself, *and if Matt doesn't show up in a few minutes, you can take off.* "Hey, weren't you supposed to be on a hot date with that Steve dude?" He had to remind himself not to call Steve "Skeeve," like he and Matt always did.

"I was," she said, forcing out a sigh. "And now I'm back."

"Oh," Jonah said. "You okay?" He pushed himself up on the counter by the stove and gave her one of his trademark half smiles.

"Yeah, I guess." Jeanie shrugged and looked down at a bulging black trash bag that sat on the floor by her feet. "I've, well . . . I've been at this for a while." She opened the top of the bag. Inside was a ton of popcorn that looked as if it had spent too much time at the tanning salon.

Jonah felt a little weird, like Jeanie was revealing a side of herself to him that he wasn't supposed to see. A screwed-up side. A side that you wouldn't expect a mother-of-two, middle school secretary to have. But it also made him feel special. That she'd trust him enough to expose herself in this way.

It was quiet. So quiet he felt as if the silence were something he could reach out and touch. Like a wool blanket wrapped tightly around his head. Jonah wanted desperately to fill the emptiness with words. Words to cheer up Jeanie. All that came to him were clichés about what she deserved and how many fish there were in the sea. He drummed his heels against the cabinet behind him, the only sound he could think to make as he racked his brain for a more original offer of comfort.

But she spoke first. "I just wanted one good batch. Except every time I try, I get to thinking and then . . ." She pointed at the stinky pot. "Sorry," she said, "I don't need to burden you with this garbage." She emptied the pot into the trash bag.

Jonah picked up a butter knife from the counter and scraped at the brown splotchy stains around one of the elements. He had two options here. He could comfort Jeanie, push her to open up, and maybe in the process learn some things about her private life he'd regret knowing. Or he could leave right now. Which is probably what he should do. But then he thought about all the times Jeanie had talked him through problems with girls, with his mom. How often she had saved him from going insane. And how maybe she didn't have anyone to keep *her* from going insane.

"It's okay," he said finally. "Tell me. I want to hear it."

Jeanie furrowed her brow, as if trying to decide whether to spill her guts. "Jonah, listen," she said. "Can I be candid?"

"Of course. I wouldn't want you any other way." He hoped she picked up on the fact that he *did* want her in some way. Well, not *really*. She was his best friend's mom after all. It's not like anything would ever actually happen. But that's exactly why flirting with Jeanie was the safest flirting possible.

"You hang out with Matty all the time," she said. "What

do you think about this business with him and Anabelle?"

"What business?" *Thank God,* Jonah thought. *This is just about Matt and Anabelle's constant fighting.* No creepy details about Jeanie's love life with Skeeve.

"Them sticking together," she said. "Long distance."

"I don't know. I mean, he loves her. He doesn't want to lose her."

"They're just out of *high school.*" Jeanie gathered the top of the popcorn bag and twisted it up as if wringing it dry. "It's not gonna last. He shouldn't expect that it will."

"Well, it probably won't. But I don't think any of us could tell them that. Isn't it something they have to figure out for themselves?" This was what he believed, and he felt wise and grown up having Jeanie consult him. But he wondered if he should've said something like, *Yeah, they should totally end it now.*

Jeanie pursed her lips into a flat line. "Anabelle's so . . . nice." She said *nice* as if it were a dirty word.

Anabelle's niceness was what Jonah liked most about her. It was what sometimes made him wish she were *his* girlfriend. He couldn't help but wonder if dating a non-needy, together girl like Anabelle would've kept him from sleeping with girls he didn't really care about. But he didn't want Jeanie to know he had any of those feelings. "Yeah, she's nice," he said, nodding. "Too nice."

"I hate to say this about my own son," Jeanie said, looking pleased that Jonah was agreeing with her, "but I think he probably doesn't deserve someone so nice. So nice and innocent." Again, she emphasized *innocent* as if it were something to be ashamed of.

Because he didn't want Jeanie to know he respected that quality in Anabelle—even envied it—he continued along the path of Anabelle-bashing. "No, I know what you mean," he said, feeling good to be able to publicly deny feelings that he was afraid had been becoming obvious. "There's something about her that's so naive. She never drinks with us or smokes up or anything. And curse words are, like, not in her vocabulary."

"Well, that's part of what concerns me," Jeanie said. "I'm afraid Matty's corrupting her. Exposing her to his vices."

That was something Jonah had wondered before, himself. He'd thought that if he were ever going to date Anabelle, it couldn't just be a one-night stand—it would have to be serious. And he'd have to give up weed and booze. Plus, more importantly, he'd have to give up his best friend. If he were going to make a move, he'd have to make sure it was absolutely the right thing.

"Actually," Jeanie continued, her voice dry and a little shrill, "what's really freaking me out is, I keep thinking maybe Matty's doing that stuff too much. But what am I gonna say? *Quit?* Right. Not when he knows I've been just as bad. When I do it with the two of you all the time."

"But it's wicked fun when you join us," Jonah told her, trying to get calm, flirty Jeanie back. "That's why you're our favorite mom."

"I am? Really?" She pulled at the wisps of hair at the back of her neck. "God, you're sweet. Men my age aren't that sweet. What happens between eighteen and thirty-five? I'd like to know." She scratched her thigh, revealing a thin web of veins, which Jonah thought was beautiful. Like blue lace.

Don't let her catch you looking, Jonah told himself. *She'll think you're a perv.* He glanced up at the strings of spaghetti stuck to the ceiling, which he and Matt had thrown there a few days ago in an attempt to see if they were done. They were all clumped together, with one dry strand dangling down, threatening to drop.

When he turned back to Jeanie, she was looking at him expectantly, as if still waiting for an answer to her seventeen-to-thirty-five question. Jonah wanted to say something witty, but the words weren't coming, so he pointed at the giant bag of popcorn. "Hey," he said a little too loudly, "when're we gonna eat that stuff already? I think I can handle half of it, but I don't know about you."

Jeanie laughed, slapping his back. "Yeah, you're right. Help me bring it in there?" She stuck her thumb out to the side, toward the living room.

"Sure . . . okay." It was one thing to shoot the shit with Jeanie alone in the kitchen. Another thing entirely to move it to the living room. That constituted actual hanging out. As in, awkwardness if Matt or Lexi came home. *Well, it's just eating popcorn,* Jonah told himself. *There's really nothing wrong with that.* He dragged the bag across the tiled floor, through the doorway, and onto the carpet.

Jeanie sat down on a small cushion that was on the floor and leaned against the bottom of the couch.

Jonah tossed off his shoes—his new favorites, the ones he'd stolen from the bowling alley—then pulled a cushion off the couch and sat a few feet away from Jeanie. He reached into the trash bag and ate a fistful of popcorn. Some of the pieces were light and fluffy—but most of them tasted a little burnt.

"How is it?" Jeanie asked hopefully.

"Pretty *good!*" Jonah said, nodding vigorously. He knew he was overdoing the enthusiasm.

"Aw, it sucks, doesn't it." Jeanie fished out a handful for herself and lifted a few kernels into her mouth with the tip of her tongue. "Crap, they really are burnt, aren't they. I knew I'd left a few batches on too long, but I didn't think it'd all be this bad." She threw what was left back into the bag and kicked it. A single kernel bounced out onto the floor.

"It's okay," Jonah said. "I like it like this. Reminds me of camping with scouts. We could never get it quite right over a real fire. It's actually kind of a nostalgic taste. Makes me feel all warm and fuzzy—like I'm about to crawl into a tent with a sleeping bag and stay up all night talking about girls."

"I'm such a bad cook," Jeanie said, pushing her head into the couch. "All I can do is microwave stuff."

"You make a mean baked potato in that microwave," Jonah assured her.

"Whatever," she said. "I bet *your* mom knows how to cook."

"Yeah, but it's all health food," Jonah said. "Everything tastes like vitamins and cardboard. Even her *cookies* have to be full of flaxseed or some weirdness."

"I don't even know what a flack seed is!"

"Trust me, Jeanie, you don't want to." Jonah reached for more popcorn. "Anyway, this stuff isn't bad. Here, I'll eat the whole thing." He leaned over the bag and shoved popcorn wildly into his mouth, Cookie Monster–style.

"Stop, stop!" Jeanie said with a snort. She covered her face with one hand and grabbed Jonah's shoulder with the other. "I can't believe that noise just came out of me!" She gave his shoulder a squeeze before letting go.

Jeanie could get pretty touchy-feely when she talked, but she'd never touched Jonah quite like that before, holding on for so long. What was that about? Probably nothing. He kept chowing on the popcorn, pretending he hadn't noticed. "Don' be 'barrassed," he told her. "*I'm* da pig! Juss loo aa me!"

"Come on!" Jeanie slapped the floor, laughing her head off. "I don't want to see you blimp out! Gotta keep that slim figure!" She touched his hand briefly.

What was going on here? Did she want something from him? Jonah dragged out his chewing, telling himself he was only imagining things. As he swallowed the last bite, Jeanie quieted down. She gave him an intense look and pinched his big toe through his sock.

Time seemed to freeze so much, he could practically feel

the popcorn stop moving down his throat. That whole thing, with the look and the toe pinch, was probably the hottest thing anyone had ever done to him. It was sexier than sex. There was no way Jeanie didn't intend for it to feel that way, right?

She lay down on the floor, repositioning the cushion under her head, still giving Jonah that *look*.

Should I give her the look back? he wondered. No, that would be crazy. Probably, he should just go home. But Jeanie was the grown-up here; she'd make sure things didn't get out of control. Right?

Just keep your face away from hers, Jonah told himself, *and everything will be fine.* He lay down on the floor, with his feet by Jeanie's head and his head by her feet. He folded his cushion and slid it under his neck.

"You're maybe the funniest guy I know, Jonah," Jeanie said, adding a grin to the look. She kicked him lightly in the chest.

The compliment made Jonah nervous, and he wasn't sure how to respond. Instead of saying anything, he caught her foot and removed her slipper. *What now?* he thought. *What do I do with my best friend's mom's bare foot?!* He brought her toes to his nose and sniffed.

"That probably stinks," Jeanie said.

Jonah rubbed his thumbs into the arch of her foot. "It does," he said. "A little. But it's a foot."

Jeanie pulled his ankles into the crook of her arm and cradled his feet against her cheek. "Why are all the good men gone?" she asked.

This is wrong, Jonah thought. *It's wrong for me to love the feeling of her warm hands through my socks, to love running my fingers over her bumpy toenails.* But he didn't stop massaging her foot. "What do you mean?" he asked, aware now that he was returning the look she'd been giving him.

"Oh, just that all the good ones," she said, wiggling her big toe in his stubble. "By my age? They're all taken. They've been snatched up by women who were much smarter than me."

"What about Steve?" Jonah asked, hoping she'd say something mean about him.

Jeanie leaned back and looked up at the ceiling. "Oh, Steve's all right," she said. "I guess we just don't want the same things anymore. Or maybe we never wanted the same things. I don't know."

"I totally know what you mean," Jonah said, clasping her foot with both hands. "That's always how it goes with me, too. It's like, you can hook up with someone, and it's wicked fun and everything, but then later on it turns into something else. Like, them wanting you to be more for them than you can be."

"Hooking up is the easy part. But finding someone you really connect with?" She pulled on the tip of his sock. "That's hard."

Jonah's breath stopped for a second. *I really should go now,* he thought. And he kept repeating those words in his head as Jeanie sat up, as she tossed her cushion next to his head, and as she lowered herself back down, propping herself up on the cushion.

Jonah flipped onto his stomach, mirroring her position. Their faces were dangerously close together.

She pushed the side of her arm gently into his. He pushed back. *Uh-oh,* he thought. *What's happening?*

"Thanks, Jonah," Jeanie said.

"For what?"

"Making me laugh tonight." She pushed harder against his arm, smiling. Two long dimples framed her mouth.

"You know what the best part about your face is?" Jonah said, praying that Matt or Lexi wouldn't walk in anytime soon.

"What?"

"Your parentheses."

"My parentheses?"

He reached over and traced each of her dimples with his finger.

Jeanie laughed quietly and lowered her head, hair falling over her eyes.

"You know what's the best part of your face?" she whispered.

Jonah shook his head. He couldn't believe she was playing along.

"Your semicolon."

"I didn't know I had one of those."

Jeanie pushed her finger into the skin just below his eye and then made a hook below it.

Jonah knew she was touching the two moles at the top of his cheek. "Well, you've also got this," he said. "But it's pretty well hidden." He placed his finger at the bridge of Jeanie's nose and slid it down to the tip. He finished with a dot on her lips.

"You're right," Jeanie said, giggling. "That exclamation point can be an elusive son of a bitch."

You have to stop this, Jonah told himself. *She's not going to. So you have to.*

"You know," Jeanie whispered. "There's a sneaky one hiding on you, too. Let's see if I can fish it out." Her eyes wandered over his face as if reading a map. "Close your eyes," she said.

Jonah shut his lids. *What is she going to do?* he thought. And why was she taking so long?

Suddenly he felt her touching the corner of his mouth. With her lips.

And then the center, then the other corner.

Three dots in a row. That was called a . . . what the hell was it called?

"Give up?" Jeanie asked.

"No, I'm, um, I'm thinking," Jonah stammered.

"I can do it again," she said.

"No, no, you don't have to. I remember."

"You can open your eyes now."

"I know. But this is helping me picture it." He didn't want to look, to see evidence of who he'd just kissed. "You know," he said, opening his eyes but keeping them off Jeanie, "I'll have to get back to you on that one." He grabbed his bowling shoes and ran for the door. "I'm sure I've got a book at home with the answer!" he yelled on his way out.

♪✳

Jonah had only gotten to the end of the Fletchers' driveway when he heard the scream.

It was deep and gravelly—kind of like a roar—and it definitely came from a female. The sound struck him in his gut, playing into all of his childhood fantasies of saving a damsel in distress. But he wasn't sure it was a role he wanted now that it could become a reality.

He tiptoed down the street in the direction of the scream, concocting a plan for how to deal with the attacker. Problem was, he didn't have anything remotely resembling a weapon. Maybe he could throw pumpkin seeds in the guy's eyes and then kick him in the nuts. Kicking in the nuts would be key.

But once he rounded the curve in the road, he saw that the screamer—who was now screaming again—was alone. And wearing an oversize red hoodie with the hood pulled all the way up. Had to be Anabelle. She'd been wearing that thing nonstop. The other day he'd put her in a headlock and made her admit it belonged to Tobin Wood. Why did girls always have a thing for dopey guys like that?

Jonah caught up with Anabelle and fell in step with her. "Well, *that* was scary," he said.

"Where'd you come from?" she asked, mildly hysterical.

"I heard you from back there," he said. "I was at Matt's."

She turned, gave him a funny look. "Matt was with me."

"Yeah, I know," he said, hoping she didn't notice the slight crack in his voice. "That's why I was leaving. Because he wasn't there."

Anabelle pulled a leaf off of a sea-rose bush along the side of the road and shredded it as she walked. "He dropped me in his driveway, then went driving off somewhere. Said he needed to think."

"What's going on?" Jonah asked.

"Stuff."

"Apparently. You wanna tell me about it?"

"Not really."

"You know what?" he said. "This is bullshit."

"What is?" Anabelle halted in her tracks, looked up at him all glassy-eyed.

"Stuff with you and Matt is getting worse and worse and you keep pretending like nothing's wrong. But something is obviously very wrong. And every time I try to tell you I'm there for you, you push me away. I give up."

"Fine," she said. "We can talk if you want to talk. But not like this. Not where we could run into people we know. We have to go somewhere. Sit down. In private."

"Okay, yeah, we can do that." Man, were things even worse than he'd thought? Was Matt hurting her? He'd kill him if he was. Jonah had never been in a fistfight, but was certain he could kick Matt's ass if it came to that. "I know the perfect place," he told her. "And it's Monday, so nobody will be there."

♪✱

WhirrrlyWorld was a cinch to break into. All you had to do was crawl under the hole in the chain-link fence over by the Salt 'n' Pepper Shake-ahhh! He and Matt had done it countless times during off-season, when they cut class to smoke up.

"Ladies first," he told Anabelle when they got to the hole.

"Wait," she said, "I have to finish this." She was eating a rosehip Jonah had picked for her on their way. He'd told her it was jam-packed with vitamin C, that maybe it would make her feel better. She'd been taking tiny little bites, making an ooh-this-is-sour face as she chewed. It was supercute.

When Anabelle had polished off her rosehip, she looked around as if gearing herself up for a heist, then wriggled her way through the hole. Jonah followed. They walked past the WhirrrlyWind roller coaster, the Sail to the Starrrs! pirate ship, and into the kiddie area.

The carousel had this way of looking magical in the moonlight—as if it were a place where dreams could come true. Or be trampled by all those horses. Maybe that's what Jonah loved so much about it. That it felt both exciting and dangerous.

Jonah leaped onto the platform and reached out to give Anabelle a hand. "Anywhere you like," he told her, as if he were a host at a restaurant.

She picked a mid-gallop purple horse with a yellow mane. Jonah got on the whinnying red-and-black one beside it.

"So," he said, once they'd settled into their saddles, "you ready to talk?"

Anabelle fidgeted with her horse's reins, her thumbs poking through holes in the wrists of her hoodie. "Matt's been . . ."

Just say it, Jonah thought. *Just say that he's been hitting you and the boy is so dead.*

She wrapped one of the reins tightly around her hand. "He's been saying he thinks there's something going on between us."

Hold on, this was about *him*? Jonah leaned his head against the brass pole. It was cold. So cold. But he stayed there anyway, the metal freezing his brain.

What do you say, what do you say? he thought. He could admit that he was attracted to her, that he found her cute and sweet. But then what? He had this feeling that if he actually got the chance to kiss her, he'd find her *too* cute and *too* sweet. Or was that just what he was telling himself because he felt wrong about kissing Matt's girlfriend? Well, he'd almost just done that with Matt's mom and he didn't seem to have a problem with it. No, that wasn't true. He had a big problem with it. God, what was happening to him? Didn't he have any morals?

Maybe that was the biggest thing holding him back here. That Anabelle, more than anyone he knew, had high morals. She was all about morals. And he couldn't stand the idea of being the one who made her question that about herself. Besides, if he made a move on her, she'd probably reject him anyway. Because she was so good. So very, very good.

Then again, she might go along with it. And if she did, it would be proof that even the most well-intentioned people have weaknesses. That she wasn't so different from him after all.

"Did you hear what I said?" she asked.

"I heard," he said, sitting back up. The cold spot on his

forehead suddenly swelled with warmth. "It's just, it's so ridiculous that he'd think that."

"That's what I told him." Was he just hearing things or did she sound disappointed?

"Right, because there's not," he said. "Anything going on, I mean."

"I know." She took a quick breath, tugged on the strings of her hood. "Hey," she said, "you're gonna see him more than I will next year. Can you, like, make sure he doesn't go crazy? Remind him that I care about him?"

"Yeah," he lied, knowing Matt would drive himself as crazy as he wanted and nobody could stop him. "I can do that."

A foghorn groaned out on the water and it reminded him of the sounds of agony he'd woken up to this morning, coming from his mother's room. He wondered what she was doing right now, if she'd really gone to the hospital. Probably. He should've been home all this time, keeping her from spending money they didn't have on treatments she didn't need.

"Jonah?" Anabelle said.

"Yeah?"

"Why're you sticking around next year?"

It was a question he asked himself every day. "I don't know," he told her. "I guess school's never been my thing. But I wonder sometimes if that was a mistake. If I should've tried harder. Maybe gone somewhere other than Normal Community."

"You still could."

"No, Anabelle, I couldn't. I'm not like you. My grades suck. And there's nothing interesting about me either. I never did an extracurricular in my life. Unless you count pot. And last time I checked with admissions people, they don't."

"Sorry, I didn't mean to push you," she said, stretching her legs out in her stirrups. "It just feels weird sometimes. Being the only one of our friends going so far from home."

"If they make you feel bad, it's 'cause they're jealous," he said. "I know I am. I like to imagine myself walking around a pretty campus, living in a dorm."

"What would you study if you went?" Her eyes were all round. Full of genuine concern, interest. She was the only person he knew who really wanted to know the answers to questions she asked.

"You'll laugh," he said.

"I won't."

He knew she wouldn't. But still, it was so hard to say aloud.

"C'mon already," she prodded.

"All right, all right. If I could be anything I wanted, I'd be an . . . engineer," he admitted.

"Wow, that's not at all what I expected," Anabelle said.

"That's why I didn't want to tell you. It sounds so nerdy, right?"

"No, it's actually really cool. It's the kind of thing I could never do. I don't have the head for it."

"When I was a kid I used to take apart my mom's vacuum cleaner. She'd yell at me, but I'd always put it back together just like I found it. I did the same thing with our phone, our radio, our clocks. I feel like if I worked really hard, I could build things from scratch. Things nobody else has ever made."

"Like what?"

He'd never told anyone the thing he *really* wanted to make. The thing he'd dreamed of making since he was ten. But Anabelle would listen; she'd take him seriously. "Wings," he said, standing up in his stirrups, holding his horse's reins. "I want to build myself wings. Mechanical wings, to wear on my back. So, y'know, I could take off whenever I wanted." He looked toward the beach and pictured himself soaring out of the park, over the sand, the rippling water.

"I like that," she said.

"Yeah? You don't think it's cheesy?"

"No, I think you should do it. Apply somewhere to transfer next year. If you write a good enough essay, maybe your grades won't matter so much."

Jonah sat back down in his saddle. He didn't want to tell her that even if he had straight A's, he didn't think he could ever stray far from Normal. Not with his mom being the way she was. He had to get off this woulda, shoulda, coulda topic; it was too depressing. "So," he said, trying to keep his voice light, "what're we gonna do about Matt? Want me to set him straight?" He struck a boxing pose.

"No," she said emphatically. "You can't tell him we talked about this."

"Yeah. You wouldn't want anything to do with me anyway," he assured her. "I'm wicked bad news."

{ HOW *to* EAT *a* CHOCOLATE BOOB }

lexi fletcher

The chocolate boob was much bigger than it had appeared to Lexi when she'd spotted it in the candy case at Normal's Naughty Nibbles. Probably a D cup. Maybe even double D. In any case, it was so gigantic that Anabelle couldn't seem to get her mouth around it. But Lexi had a sinking feeling there was more than the size of the thing that was keeping Anabelle from eating it.

Anabelle put the boob back down on the kitchen island,

its bottom smacking against the wooden countertop. "I just can't stop thinking about what it is," she said.

"It's your favorite food," Lexi shot back.

"What it *looks* like."

"C'mon, you prude, you know you want it."

Anabelle rolled her eyes. Lexi took Anabelle's eye rolls as an extreme compliment. She only gave them to people she knew well—and they were specially reserved for things that really got under her skin. Calling her a prude, a kiss-up, anything that made her sound like a good girl, always worked.

Anabelle sighed and gingerly lifted the boob again. "It's heavy," she said.

"It's solid chocolate." Lexi sang the words, trying to make it sound more appealing.

"*Milk* chocolate." Anabelle giggled. Good. Giggling was a good sign.

"Don't suck too hard or you'll drain it all out!" Lexi joked.

Anabelle doubled over laughing, being careful not to drop the boob. It was one of her incredible deep hyperventilating laughs that she only did when she honestly thought something was funny. This was the goofy Anabelle that Lexi loved—the Anabelle who'd improvised a scene with her in theater class about a chameleon complaining to a shrink about how he can't stop blending in. The Anabelle who used to hang out with Lexi every day after school until her brother swooped in and somehow made himself Anabelle's Boyfriend For Life.

"Okay," Anabelle said, mid-laugh, "I'm going for it." She held the boob up to her face as if it were a mirror, then stuck the nipple between her teeth and bit, snapping off the rounded chocolate nub.

"Man, I can't believe you went straight for the nipple!" Lexi cried.

Anabelle put the boob back on the counter. "What was I *supposed* to do?" she asked, examining her melty-chocolate-covered palms. "It's the only part sticking out!"

"Even so!" Lexi said, grabbing one of Anabelle's gloppy hands. "Don't you want to save the best for last?" She leaned in and sucked the chocolate off of Anabelle's thumb with her best approximation of over-the-top movie-star sexiness. "What kind of lesbian *are* you?"

Anabelle stared at the finger that was covered in Lexi's saliva. That lesbian comment seemed to be sticking with her. But Lexi couldn't tell from Anabelle's squinty-eyed face what she was thinking.

This was a flawed plan, Lexi thought. *It was never going to work.* As if eating a chocolate boob was really going to lead to an honest conversation about how nice real boobs were, and about everything that had been on Lexi's mind for the last year and a half.

Anabelle's jaw came unhinged, as if she was about to ask a question. But all she could get out was "Are—" before the phone rang.

Of course, it was Matt. And of course he wanted to talk to Anabelle. And of course he was pissed at her over God knows what.

As if Matt had anything to be pissed about. For the past week he'd been in Boston with their dad, finding an apartment for next year. Their dad had insisted that Matt not go to college right away, that he have some "much-deserved time off." Whatever that meant. Dad always gave them whatever they wanted. As if trampolines, electric guitars, or city apartments could make up for his leaving them for Bridget, the Swedish au pair who used to vacation with them here—back when the Normal house was just their summer place.

Lexi stomped into the living room and threw herself on the couch.

Through the doorway, she could hear Anabelle's bummed-out *mm-hmm*s and desperate *no, I love you*s. It was hard to make out exactly what else she was saying, but it sounded like she was defending herself.

Lexi didn't even realize she'd been nervously rooting around between the couch cushions until her hand came upon something that crunched against her fingers. It turned out to be a piece of grody brownish popcorn. Man, her brother was a slob. She'd been finding random pieces of popcorn all over the living room lately.

Suddenly, over in the kitchen, Anabelle's voice rose and Lexi distinctly heard, "How many times do I have to tell you? We're just friends."

Lexi shot straight up. Was it possible, she wondered, that Anabelle was talking about *her*?

For over a year now there had been rumors circulating that Lexi was a lesbian. She'd often heard her nickname, *Lexbian*, whispered or fake-coughed as she walked down the halls. At first she'd chalked it up to catty girls being jealous over a starring role going to a sophomore. But the thing was, the more she thought about it, the more Lexi wondered if maybe the rumors were true. Yeah, she found girls attractive. But she also found guys attractive. She'd never kissed a boy, only a girl—a girl with freckles on her lips named Jamie. That was back in eighth grade at drama camp. They hadn't labeled it as anything. Not dating, not fooling around even. It was just something they did as part of their hanging out. And it wasn't something they'd had to talk about to know they wanted to do it; they both just knew.

Lexi had never gotten a vibe like that from any other girl. Until she'd met Anabelle. Anabelle almost always chose to sleep in Lexi's bed when she stayed over, even though Lexi's mom wouldn't have cared if she stayed with Matt. Plus, Anabelle had recently confided in Lexi about how fooling around with Matt was no fun anymore. How he always wanted stuff done to him but never offered to do stuff for her. That was what Lexi didn't get about the appeal of being with a guy. Their parts seemed to be designed precisely to do things to you, not with you. But most girls seemed to think that was just fine, even desirable. Was something wrong with Lexi for not agreeing? She needed to know that there wasn't.

Another "I love you" from the kitchen. Along with a "No, don't say that. We'll figure this out. We *will*."

There was no time for this. Matt would be coming home in less than twenty-four hours. That meant less than twenty-four hours of one-on-one time with Anabelle. Less than twenty-four hours for Lexi to figure out how to start this very important conversation. And the more Matt dragged Anabelle down, the harder it would be to say, "Hey, I know this is gonna sound weird, but I think I like girls . . . and, uh, I think maybe you do, too."

Anabelle was busy giving Matt the longest-drawn-out goodbye in history. *Just hang up!* Lexi thought. She strutted back toward the kitchen, singing "So Long, Farewell" from *The Sound of Music*. It seemed to be working—a few lines in, she heard the click of the phone hanging up. She hopped toward the doorway, still singing, and tried to think of a way to pick up where they'd left off. But when she leaped over the threshold, it was clear that that wouldn't happen for a while.

Anabelle was standing in front of the boob with a meat cleaver. In one fell swoop, she chopped the boob in half. And she kept hacking away, hunks of chocolate flying everywhere. She was wielding the knife so recklessly, it looked like she was bound to chop off one of her fingers.

"Stop it!" Lexi yelled at the top of her lungs. "Stop it, stop it, stop it!"

Anabelle threw the knife down and jumped away, pressing her back against the refrigerator, as if the knife might suddenly lunge at her of its own free will. She was making a hyperventilating sound, kind of like her laugh, but this time it was because she was gulping back sobs.

Lexi had never seen Anabelle cry before. It was scary to watch. But it was also sort of a relief to know that she did sometimes.

♪✳

As they washed up that night, Anabelle's spirits seemed to be a bit higher. They'd just finished playing one of their favorite games. A game they'd made up, which involved Anabelle pounding out show tunes from Lexi's Broadway book and Lexi making up funny, often dirty lyrics about kids at school. She went after the jocks, the art kids, the loners. Even the Players weren't safe.

"You're such a good pianist," Lexi told Anabelle after spitting a foamy glob of toothpaste down the drain. "You're totally gonna go pro."

"Maybe." Anabelle shrugged, then splashed water over her soapy face. "Maybe you will, too."

"No, you're way out of my league. Sure, I'm good here in Normal. But if we'd stayed in Boston, I never could've gotten a leading role."

Anabelle unscrewed a bottle of facial toner and began to apply it with a cotton pad on her clear-to-the-point-of-translucent skin.

"Can you skip the face routine tonight?" Lexi asked,

stretching and faking a yawn. "I'm sleepy." Really, she was wired—she felt like she did right before the premiere performance of a play—but she wanted to get to bed already. She figured that lying down with the lights out would create the right atmosphere to finally bring up what she needed to get off her chest.

"I already started," Anabelle said. "It won't take long."

Lexi was tempted to call her Face Geek or something to get an eye roll. But she didn't want to risk pissing her off right now. She sat on the side of the tub and watched Anabelle circle the cotton pad over her cheeks. She looked like a kid, standing on her toes even though she was tall enough to see the mirror. The pose made her calf muscles all taut just below the hem of her nightgown.

"You've got the best legs," Lexi said. She was afraid she'd sounded more jealous than wistful.

"They're just legs."

"But they're shaped nicely."

"What do you mean? They're leg-shaped."

"No, look at mine." Lexi held out one of her legs. "They're all skinny and deflated-looking."

"Isn't skinny what most girls want to be?"

God, why couldn't Anabelle ever accept flattery? All she needed to do was say thank you. "You can't ever take a compliment, can you?" Lexi said, wishing the words hadn't come out so accusatory.

"That's not true, I can," Anabelle said, her lips getting pouty.

"No. You can't," Lexi said. "You're pretty lucky, you know. You've got curls I'd kill for, you've actually got curves. You're the best pianist in the state—and that's not even subjective. You were actually rated number one by real judges."

Anabelle closed her toner bottle tightly and popped open the cap of her moisturizer. She squirted some in her palm and rubbed it into her cheeks in tiny circular motions. Lexi was sure she was going extra slowly just to agitate her. *Great*, she thought. *Now you've gotten her all tense.*

"You've got money," Anabelle said, making eye contact with Lexi through the mirror. "You don't have to put on an apron and bonnet every summer and work at the freaking taffy shop, where they're so old-timey they don't believe in air-conditioning. You don't have to think about how maybe you won't get to be a musician because you'll be paying off your student loans for eternity. And probably supporting your parents on top of it all."

Lexi didn't want to argue anymore, but there was no way Anabelle could've said that without knowing it would sting.

"Yeah, and you know why I have money?" Lexi asked.

"Yes," Anabelle said with a sigh, "I do."

"I'd trade it all in a second for what you've got. You're the only person I know who doesn't have a fucked-up family."

Anabelle didn't have anything to say to that. She didn't even give an eye roll. In fact, what she did was way worse than an eye roll: she completely avoided looking at Lexi. And she kept up her silent treatment until they finally climbed into bed.

♪❋

It was one of those rare sticky nights when it was too hot for covers. Still, Lexi liked the comfort of having a sheet on top of her, and Anabelle usually did, too—but tonight she wouldn't get inside. She curled up in fetal position, her back to Lexi.

Lexi stared out her window, up at the sky. The clouds looked like tiny puffs of smoke. There was a group of them all bunched up like a hat over the moon and one right below them, like a lone eyebrow.

"We okay?" she asked Anabelle, desperate for things to get back to normal.

"I guess," Anabelle said unconvincingly.

"I'm sorry I got bitchy."

Anabelle rolled onto her back. "It's okay," she said.

"I just admire you so much. And it felt like you were rejecting me."

"Sorry, I didn't mean to be like that. I guess I just don't think of myself in those ways that you were describing me."

"Well, whether you see it or not, it's all true."

"Thanks, that's nice of you to say."

If Lexi strained her ears, she could hear waves crashing in the distance. They fell in patterns. A few at a time in quick succession, then a long period of silence before a huge one rolled in. She wondered if the air had been cleared enough to tell Anabelle what was on her mind. Maybe they could start by playing that game where they gave each other the shivers. Anabelle always seemed to like that.

Lexi lay there, the chant running through her mind:

> *Crack an egg on your head,*
> *Let the yolk run down,*
> *Let the yolk run up,*
> *Let the yolk run down.*

The last time they'd played, Lexi had pulled her nightgown over her head and held it in front of her chest while Anabelle ran her fingers over Lexi's bare back and arms. And then, to Lexi's surprise, Anabelle had done the same with

her nightgown. Lexi had gone extra slow to prolong touching Anabelle's smooth skin.

> *Squeeze oranges on your shoulders,*
> *Let the juice run down,*
> *Let the juice run up,*
> *Let the juice run down.*

Yes, that's exactly what we should do, Lexi thought. *We should
play that.* But all she did was keep silently reciting the
words to herself.

> *Stab a knife in your back,*
> *Let the blood drip down,*
> *Let the blood drip up,*
> *Let the blood drip down.*

> *Crisscross applesauce,*
> *Spiders running up and down . . .*

No, she thought before she even got to the end. *This isn't
right. It'll take too long.* At this late stage it was probably best
to be direct. Maybe start by admitting to Anabelle that she'd
lied about losing her virginity during her trip to Boston

last summer, that there was no hot coffee-shop guy named Jamie. That, yes, there was a Jamie, but Lexi had known this person a couple years ago and not from Boston and they hadn't actually *done it* and, and, and . . . she was a girl. Yes, a girl.

Maybe Anabelle would be intrigued, would have questions about it. And maybe she'd admit that she'd always wondered what kissing a girl would be like. Maybe she'd want to try it. Or just lie there holding each other.

Or maybe she'd never want to talk to Lexi again.

But maybe that didn't matter—she'd be leaving in a month anyway. There wasn't really anything to lose. Except, of course, if she really did keep dating Matt forever and ever. And then they'd be in the same family. And boy, would that be awkward.

Lexi tried to come up with the right words. She tried to memorize them. But she had to memorize them in such a way that when they came out they'd sound spontaneous, as if this thought had just occurred to her, as if it hadn't been weighing on her constantly.

Just as she felt ready to say something, Anabelle got out of bed.

"Where you going?" Lexi asked.

"Bathroom," Anabelle answered in a tone that said, *What's it to you?*

Okay, Lexi thought. *When she gets back. No more excuses.*

Minutes passed. Many minutes. More minutes than it should take to go to the bathroom, no matter what you were doing in there. Lexi listened for a flush. She didn't hear one. But she did hear voices. Hushed voices, coming from her mom's room. She tiptoed down the hall and stood by the cracked-open door.

"It's so confusing," she heard Anabelle say. "I just don't know what to do."

"Well, I'm not going to tell you to break up with Matty or not—that's your decision," Lexi's mom said.

Wow, Lexi thought, *she's really going to end it.* She was tempted to bust into the room and start jumping on the bed like she did when she was a kid, back when her parents were still together.

"But if you do break up with him," her mom continued, "which I think is fine, it should be because it feels like that's what has to happen. Not because you're curious about someone else."

Curious about someone else? What? Was Anabelle really telling Lexi's mom about this? About what was going on between the two of them? How embarrassing. She didn't want her mom to know about that. Not yet, at least. At the same time, it was a relief to know Anabelle was feeling just as confused as she was. She had to get Anabelle out of there so they could discuss this privately.

"And besides," her mom added, "I can't really see you and Jonah together anyway. He's too tall for you."

The words hit Lexi like a bowling ball in the stomach. Anabelle had been talking about Jonah. Not her. Of course she had. They'd been flirting like crazy lately, but then, Jonah flirted like crazy with everyone. But she'd been an idiot not to have seen it for what it was.

Anabelle was heterosexual, just like everyone else. Every one else except Lexi, who was the only girl in this town to ever be a maybe, probably lesbian.

Lexi needed some air.

She ran down the stairs and practically bashed right into—surprise, surprise—Jonah, who was heading up as she was heading down.

"When did you . . . what're you . . ." she started asking, not sure what her question was. Her head was all over the place. It felt like it was crawling with ants.

Jonah's face turned the color of that ugly hoodie Anabelle had been wearing lately. "Whoops," he said, running back downstairs. "Forgot Matt was still gone. I'll come back tomorrow."

"Liar," Lexi said, leaning over the banister to keep herself steady. "Why'd you really come?" *Just say it*, she thought. *Say you came for Anabelle.*

"Actually," he said walking up to her. "I came for you." Another lie. He never came looking for her.

"Yeah, right."

"Well, for you and Anabelle."

Now we're getting somewhere, Lexi thought.

"I wondered if . . . if maybe you wanted to break into one of the McMansion pools," Jonah said. "I found a wicked cool one last night on my way home from a party."

She could tell he was making this up as he went along, but the excitement of trespassing actually sounded good right now. A much-needed release. "Yeah, let's do it," she said. "Hang on, I just have to get Anabelle."

"She sleeping?"

"No, she's in my mom's room. Having some sort of heart-to-heart."

"Oh yeah? What about?"

"Boys, what else?"

Jonah shifted on his feet and rubbed his hand nervously through his five-o'clock shadow. Lexi got why he was jittery; it was the same reason she had been, just minutes ago.

She decided right then: there was no way she was letting Jonah and Anabelle be alone tonight. If she couldn't have what she wanted, then neither could they.

♪﹡

Lexi had thought she'd never find herself in a stranger pool than the heart-shaped one last summer that belonged to the couple with an unusually large collection of miniature poodles. But this one that Jonah took them to was definitely weirder. In fact, the only thing that tipped her off to knowing that this little body of water was, in fact, a swimming pool was the diving board on the end. Otherwise, it looked like a pond. Instead of concrete around the edge, there was slate and the sides were made of varying levels of smooth rocks.

The house itself was pretty spooky. It looked like an old castle, even though it was brand-new. And there were giant bushes cut to look like animals all over the lawn. The whole place felt like a movie set, which Lexi found sort of fitting. She had a sense that something dramatic was going to happen tonight and this seemed like the perfect setting for things to go down.

The three of them stood at the foot of the pool, checking to make sure nobody was watching them. All of the lights in the house seemed to be out, which either meant the people who lived there weren't around or they were asleep. It was always better to err on the safe side and keep quiet. Which was also way more exciting.

Jonah untied his shoes and threw them into the grass, then tossed off his shirt and shorts until he was just in his boxers. He lowered himself into the water on the long wide rocks arranged like steps. Lexi was going back and forth over whether or not to go in in her clothes. She was starting to regret having laughed at Anabelle back at the house for saying she didn't want to go swimming because she didn't have a bathing suit. The truth was, even though Lexi wore bikinis, she hated them because they made her lack of womanly features so clear.

She looked over at Anabelle, who was unbuckling her sandals at a glacial pace. And as uncomfortable as Lexi was with her body, it occurred to her that right now she had the opportunity to make Anabelle look like a wuss in front of Jonah. She tore her clothes off as quickly as possible and stepped into the lukewarm water in her bra and underwear.

Even though it was dark and she was pretty sure nobody could see anything, she had to fight an urge to cross her arms over her chest. She ducked down, making sure the water covered her shoulders. *You're in a show right now,* she told herself. A show starring a fearless heroine who didn't give a damn if anyone saw her in her soaked, natural-color bra.

Anabelle walked up to the edge of the pool and curled her toes over the slate. The spot between her eyebrows was all wrinkly.

"What's your problem?" Lexi whispered up to her.

"I'm not stripping," Anabelle clipped back. It seemed like she didn't want Jonah to hear.

Jonah waded over to them. "She need a push?" he asked Lexi with a grin.

"She needs some guts," Lexi answered.

Anabelle crouched down. "What'd you say?" she challenged.

"Anabelle," Lexi said. "You're so amazing. But you know what would make you even more amazing?"

"What," Anabelle said, through clenched teeth.

"If you'd just take a risk once in your life."

Major eye roll.

Lexi knew she'd won a point there, but this one didn't make her feel good.

"Ladies, hey, this is supposed to be fun." Jonah stuck his face in Anabelle's. "Look, here's what we'll do," he said. "Lexi and I will go underwater for, like, ten seconds. That's how long you've got to get in."

"Or what?" Anabelle said, all sassy.

"You don't want to find out," Jonah flirted back.

"Maybe I do," Anabelle said, hands on her hips.

Jonah turned to Lexi, gave her a nod, and disappeared underwater. Lexi followed his lead and began to count Mississippis. She was sure this was a ploy to get her out of the picture for a brief moment while the two of them made out. She came up two seconds early, convinced she'd catch them with their lips locked. But all she saw was Anabelle sitting on the side of the pool with her feet dangling in the water. Still fully clothed.

Jonah's head surfaced all the way in the deep end. He shook out his hair like a wet dog, then spotted Anabelle across the water. "You're gonna regret this, Seulliere," he said quietly, swimming the crawl over to her.

"Wait," Anabelle said when he was about a foot away. "I just need to know something."

Jonah glided up and wrapped his hands around her ankles. "Make it quick," he said, giving her feet a tug. "Lexi and I have to take care of your punishment."

Lexi hoped Anabelle's punishment didn't involve getting out of the pool.

Anabelle braced herself, gripping the slate. "Why'd you come over so late while Matt was gone?" she asked Jonah.

Jonah pushed his legs out behind him and flutter-kicked to keep himself afloat. "I don't know," he said. "Habit, I guess."

Anabelle dipped her hand in the water and spritzed Jonah in the face.

What's she doing? Lexi wondered. He wasn't going to admit he'd come over to see her. Not with Lexi right there.

"You know what?" he said, creeping his fingers like tarantulas over the backs of Anabelle's legs. "I came over because I had something to say."

"Yeah?" Anabelle sounded hopeful, as if she knew deep down that this big thing Jonah had to say was for her ears. Lexi felt invisible. As if they didn't notice that she was right there, practically naked beside them. Part of her wanted to jump out of the pool and run away and another part wanted to barge in between them and push them apart.

"If you must know, I had to tell Jeanie something," Jonah said, dropping his feet and standing.

"Jeanie?" Anabelle sounded shocked.

Yeah, Lexi thought. *Jeanie? What'd you want with her at two in the morning?*

"She's been giving me advice about this situation I'm in." Jonah turned around with his back to Anabelle and bowed down, placing her feet over his chest. "Or *was* in."

"Why is my mom everyone's therapist?" Lexi asked. But she was relieved in a way that his goal hadn't been to find Anabelle. Or was this just some crazy excuse to hide that?

"So," Jonah said, ignoring Lexi, "I've kinda been seeing this woman. An older woman. Well, not *seeing* her exactly. It's complicated. Anyway. I got the good sense to realize it was no good for me. I came to tell Jeanie that."

"How old?" Anabelle asked, scrunching her nose.

"Too old." He grabbed Anabelle's hands and put them on his head. "Now hop on before I drag you in against your will."

Anabelle slid off the side of the pool onto his shoulders. She steadied herself as Jonah carried her out to the center of the water.

Lexi couldn't get Anabelle's judgmental look out of her

head. So what if Jonah was seeing an older woman? Big deal. It wasn't something to make faces about. Lexi was glad she hadn't made her confession earlier; she didn't think she could've handled Anabelle making a similar face when she found out Lexi used to make out with a girl.

Jonah walked deeper and deeper. When the water was up to his chest, Anabelle leaned over and whispered something in his ear, which Lexi couldn't hear but made Jonah smile. And then Anabelle raised her arms and started flapping them gracefully, as if she were an exotic bird. Jonah bobbed up and down along with her movements.

What in the world was going on here? Some crazy mating ritual? Watching this thing between the two of them unfold made Lexi feel sick to her stomach, like she did that time when Anabelle's boss was out of the shop and they overloaded on saltwater taffy. "Are you guys, like, practicing for some sort of two-person winged dragon role in a play I don't know about?" Even as Lexi asked it, she knew she was talking too loudly.

Anabelle and Jonah both shushed her.

Jonah turned around and glided back toward Lexi. She suddenly noticed how hairy his chest was. Much hairier than last summer. Not beastly or anything. But for the first time she thought of him as a man, not a boy.

Were she and Anabelle women? Anabelle showed more signs of becoming one than Lexi did, but flapping around up there in her dry clothes on Jonah's bare wet shoulders, she looked really young. Lexi felt relieved that Anabelle hadn't taken off her clothes; it would've felt too bad to see the two of them this close together in just undergarments, with her off to the side feeling like the only one who was still a child.

Just then, Jonah gave a big jump and dunked Anabelle underwater. There was kicking and shoving, spluttering, and the holding in of laughter.

Lexi couldn't bear to watch this any longer. She swam out to the deepest part of the deep end and wondered what would happen first: her arms and legs losing strength from treading water or Anabelle and Jonah finally giving in and kissing. *Maybe you should just get out and go home,* she thought. *Leave them to do whatever they're gonna do. It's inevitable.*

And then.

A light came on.

In the humongous corner windows on the third floor.

"You guys!" Lexi whisper-shouted. "Someone's awake in there. I think we should go."

"What," Anabelle said, clinging to Jonah's back, "so now you're suddenly not a risk taker?"

"Ouch," Jonah said with a smirk.

"Really?" Lexi said. "You really want to go there?"

"You're just always making me feel so lame and timid. I figured a little light in a house wouldn't scare you. Someone probably just got up to go to the bathroom."

Lexi's body felt like a teakettle just before it whistles, the bubbles rippling through her limbs. "Look at me, Anabelle," she said through her teeth. "Take a good hard look." She swam over to the side of the pool, kicking with all her might, and hoisted herself out. She stormed around the corner and mounted the diving board.

Anabelle was still wrapped around Jonah's back, her chin hanging over his shoulder. Her hair was sopping wet, her cheeks flushed. She looked beautiful. Lexi used to think she was the only one who could make Anabelle look like that. But right now, all Lexi was doing was making Anabelle's eyes pop.

"I am in my underwear!" Lexi said, not really caring if her voice was the teensiest bit too loud. "You've got all your clothes on." She walked out to the edge of the diving board and leaned forward to be sure Anabelle heard this next part. "You will never, ever be as daring as I am. You're afraid. Afraid to do what you know you have to do. Afraid to give in to your feelings, to go after what you want." Lexi hated herself as she was saying these things, but she felt that she had to keep going. She was a boulder halfway down a mountain in a landslide. "Why don't you two just—"

Before she could suggest that Anabelle and Jonah just get it over with already and do it, Jonah threw Anabelle off his back. "Shit!" he said. "Someone's coming!"

Lexi turned to see a girl—or woman? it was hard to tell—walking cautiously toward the pool. Anabelle and Jonah started scrambling out of the water, but Lexi didn't wait for them. She sprinted over the lawn to the staircase and down to the beach, leaving her clothes behind. She ran against the wind, letting it blow against her stomach, her face. The last time she felt this electrified she'd been onstage, zipping around in the Peter Pan flying contraption.

She turned around for a second and got a glimpse of Anabelle and Jonah, two human-shaped specks just making it onto the sand.

They would never catch up to her.

{ **ONE** *Last* **TIME** }

matt fletcher

As soon as Matt's dad dropped him off at home, he set out on his mission. His mission to find Anabelle. To see her, to hold her, to feel her squeeze his hand three times—their secret silent code for *I love you.*

The first floor was empty. Unless you counted the smell of his mom's way-too-strong coffee. Good, that meant she'd probably stayed here last night. He hoped that was a sign it was over with her and Skeeve. There had been rumblings recently about a possible engagement—how he was finally ready to commit to her. But Matt didn't buy that for a second. Guys like Skeeve didn't commit to anyone but themselves.

Matt went to the basement door and listened. No piano music; Anabelle must not be down there. As he ran up to his room, his stomach started to feel all whirry, like it did last week when he'd spun too fast on the Tipsy Teacups. Lately he'd had this feeling that something was going on between Anabelle and Jonah; over the weekend he'd convinced himself that it was probably true. And the longer it took him to find her, the more sure he became that it was absolutely, positively, without-a-doubt true. *Please let her be sitting on my bed waiting for me,* he thought. *Please, please, please.*

She wasn't.

He banged on Lexi's door and didn't even wait for her groggy "Yeah?" before busting in.

Lexi was lying there, all tangled up in her sheet. It was one o'clock—why wasn't she up yet? She was usually driving him crazy with her operatic shower singing by at least ten.

"Where's Anabelle?" he demanded, as if he were a detective and Lexi was a criminal hiding Anabelle away in an undisclosed location.

"I don't know," Lexi said, blinking her bleary eyes. "She never came back."

"Came back from where?" Oh God, he was right. She was out fooling around with Jonah.

"*No*where," Lexi said with melodramatic exasperation. "She just . . . she left early. Really early."

"But it's her day off," he said, dumbfounded. "She knew I was coming home today."

Lexi rolled over and put a pillow over her head. Big help she was.

Matt ran back downstairs, imagining all the different places where Anabelle and Jonah might be making out: on the beach, on the jetty, in the back room at the taffy shop.

He paced around the kitchen island. It was covered in smashed bits of chocolate. His mom always overdid it on the chocolate when she was having man issues.

On his third time around, he grabbed a cantaloupe from the fruit bowl and tossed it back and forth between his palms. *Where could they be, where could they be, where could they be?* Maybe they were hanging out on the swing set in Anabelle's yard. On, like, a real date. Which somehow felt even worse than if they were groping in a closet.

Matt had been right. He'd been right all along to not want to leave them alone. Why hadn't Anabelle come with him to Boston? She could've taken a few days off from work. He'd even offered to give her the money she'd be losing. There was only one answer to why she didn't take him up on it, and that was Jonah. It had to be.

Matt raced out the back door, forgetting he was still holding the cantaloupe. But, *agh*, there was no time to bring it back inside. He smashed it in the driveway, the orange flesh exploding on the pavement like a Jackson Pollock painting.

There's gotta be a metaphor there, Matt thought, staring at the cracked-open, bald-headed melon. Something about destroyed innocence? He made a mental note to remember that for tonight when he smoked up and started writing. Which he actually hadn't done in a few days; his dad didn't allow pot at his place. And Matt couldn't write without being stoned. Or not his really deep stuff anyway. He had so much buzzing around in his head, he couldn't wait to get it all out. So much that maybe the best way to express it would be with a gigantic paintbrush. Or a wet ball of clay. It was always so hard to choose the right medium.

First, though, he had to get this Anabelle-and-Jonah thing settled.

Matt bolted out to the street, not sure where he was heading, but knowing he had to find them. And boy, were they going to be sorry when he did. As he bounded toward the street, he felt strong. He felt like the Incredible Hulk becoming big and green.

He looked back at the cantaloupe brains.

Yes, they were going to be sorry.

♪✳

When Matt got to Anabelle's house, her dad was lying in a half-full kiddie pool reading the paper.

"Hey, Karl," Matt said, trying to hide his post-run wheezing. "Anabelle home?"

Karl jolted up, the bottom half of his paper dipping into the shallow water. "Matt!" he cried, messily folding the unwieldy pages. "Long time no see! Yeah, she's up in her room practicing. Go on in!"

"She by herself?"

"Yeah, the girls are out with Marnie." Karl lifted the brim of his sweat-stained, sun-bleached Normal baseball cap and faked a menacing look. "But I'm not budging, so don't you go trying anything."

"I won't." He really wouldn't. Anabelle had never felt comfortable messing around in her room. She said it was too weird to do stuff right near where her sisters slept. And aside from that, her place was so small and old you could hear every little creak no matter where you were in the house.

Matt climbed the stairs, relieved to know Anabelle was home. And alone.

He found her sitting on her perfectly made bed under her poster of Thelonious Monk in a kids' wagon. She was hunched over the keyboard with big bulky headphones plugged into a Walkman—who used a Walkman anymore?—wearing that baggy red hoodie of hers, the one she'd stolen from her dad. When she saw Matt she stopped playing and pulled off the headphones. But she didn't come to greet him. No hugs. Just a quick "Hi."

Well, no hugs from him then, either. Matt sat down on the corner of the bed. "What're you playing?" he asked.

"It's Schubert," she said. "Piano Trio in B-flat."

"Anabelle," he said, scooting closer to her on the bed. "When—" No, he couldn't just ask her when she was going to start being honest with him. When she was going to come clean about whatever the hell was going on with Jonah. If he just accused her, she'd never open up. *You've gotta lead up to it,* he told himself.

"When what?" she asked, her eyes getting squinty.

"When are you going to start playing meaningful stuff?"

It was unrelated to Jonah, but something he'd wanted to bring up with her for a long time.

"What're you talking about?" She swallowed hard. "This *is* meaningful. To me, it is."

"But I mean, when are you going to start composing? Making your own music?" He hit one of the black keys sharply and she flinched. "That's why I got you this thing."

"I don't know," she said, shutting off the keyboard. "I'm not really interested in that." She held up the Walkman. "When I figure out stuff, I almost feel like I did create it."

"But it's like if I copied a Van Gogh, instead of trying to *be* the next Van Gogh. You could be the next Van Gogh, too, but for piano." He could tell he was making her feel bad. But in a way, he felt that she deserved it. Because even though she wasn't with Jonah right now, she'd definitely been all over him lately. And was probably out late doing God-knows-what with him last night. And that was not how a girlfriend should behave with her boyfriend's best friend.

Anabelle inhaled so hard he could hear her nose whistling. She looked out her window, then back at him, then up at the ceiling, then out the window again. She got up and shot over to her sisters' beds and curled up on the bottom bunk, hugging an enormous pink stuffed rabbit—one of the many animals Anabelle's dad bragged about winning for her at balloon darts when she was a kid. She buried her face in the bunny's matted fur and started to sob. "I think we should maybe . . ."

"Speak up," he said, raising his hand to his ear. "You think we should maybe what?"

She pulled the rabbit away from her lips and looked him dead in the eye. "Maybe break up, Matt. Okay? Was that loud enough for you?"

Wait, wait, wait. Break up? *Break up?* This wasn't supposed to happen. He was supposed to get mad at her; she was supposed to apologize. And then things were supposed to get back to the way they were. They weren't supposed to end. And even if they did, it wasn't supposed to be her dumping *him*. Back when they'd started dating, he could've had his pick of girls, but she was nobody—a loner. Now, just because some other dude was paying attention to her, she thought she was better than him?

He tried to make his voice steady, calm. Calm enough to make her see that he could be rational, that breaking up was not the answer. "You have to tell me what happened."

"Nothing happened," she insisted, tears rolling down the sides of her nose.

"If you're saying you want to split up, something definitely happened."

Anabelle squeezed the rabbit against her chest and sniffled. "You wouldn't understand."

"I'll kick his ass." Matt rose to his feet and slammed his foot into the bed frame. "I swear to God." He didn't really intend to fight Jonah—Jonah was bigger and would probably beat Matt. But he liked that when he said it, it sounded like he meant it. Like he was a guy who could actually pull off that kind of thing.

"Don't," Anabelle said, now full-on crying. "Please."

"Then tell me." Matt sat back down beside her and she pulled back slightly. *Wow, she's afraid of me,* he thought. Good, maybe she'd quit whatever was going on with Jonah.

"All that happened," she said, staring him down with her red-rimmed eyes, "is Jonah and I snuck into one of the McMansion pools."

"I knew it," he snapped.

"Lexi was there, too," she added quickly. "The three of us went."

"And . . .?"

"And nothing. We swam, someone came out of the house, we left."

"Then what? Lexi says you never came back."

"Well . . . yeah." Anabelle backed slowly into the pile of stuffed animals in the corner behind her. "Lexi took off," she said. "And Jonah and I hung out on the beach for a while talking. Just talking, that was it."

"And that's what convinced you you should dump me?"

"No. It's actually something I've been thinking about. Maybe talking to Jonah helped me to see things more clearly. But I promise, I'm not dumping you for him. It's not like that."

"You're attracted to him, though."

"No." She said it so emphatically it had to be a lie.

"Come on, admit it. It's obvious."

"Okay, yeah, if that's what you want to hear, I think he's good-looking and all that. I'd be lying if I said I didn't. Everyone does." She was clenching and unclenching her fists. Her knuckles were white. Four white mountain peaks. Plus the sad thumb knuckle, all low and rounded and off on its own. "Matt, I wouldn't be doing this if it was just about having a fling with someone else," she said, looking down at her feet. Her toes were curled under. They had knuckles, too. *There should really be a poem about knuckles,* he thought. *How they're a reflection of our emotions.* "It's about you and me," she continued. "And I can't do it anymore."

She burst out crying again. Hard. There was heaving and wailing and snotty snorting. "This is the hardest thing in the world I've ever had to do. Can't you see that?"

The crying was either a manipulative way to cover for cheating on him, or she was telling the truth about Jonah. The way she was bawling right now, he kind of believed her. But still, even if nothing physical had happened, Matt couldn't help feeling like Jonah must've said something to make her want to end things. Why else would she suddenly decide to do this? There had to be more to it than what she was telling him. In one way or another, there had been a betrayal.

"You know what?" he said. "People don't cry like this. They don't cry like this unless someone died." He realized as he said it that he was repeating something his father had told him during the divorce. It was something that had just made him cry harder, and it had the same effect on Anabelle.

God, this was a mess. He needed a drink. A hit. Lots of hits. How had things gotten this bad? Did they really have to break up? He didn't want to. He wanted to tell her he was sorry. For whatever he had done. For getting her so worked up. He couldn't imagine life without her.

He wrapped his arms around her shaking shoulders, pulled her head to his chest, rubbed his fingers against the ridge on the back of her skull the way she liked. He felt her muscles relax a bit. "You really want to break up?" he asked.

She nodded and barely audibly said, "I think so."

"Is there anything I can do to change your mind?"

"Probably not."

"It's just, it's a big decision. One we shouldn't make so quickly." Matt looked her in the eye, wiped away her tears with his thumbs. "Look, I know I'm an asshole sometimes. I can work on that."

He offered her the bottom of his shirt to blow her nose into. The snot came out all clear and a little bubbly. He told himself to remember later to cut out that bit of the fabric once it had crusted up and use it in a collage.

"This sucks," she said. "I don't know what to do."

Good, it sounded like her mind wasn't totally made up. He had to get out of this room, though. Someplace where he wasn't being watched by teddy bears and figurines and other cute little-girl things. "Can we, like, go for a walk or something?" he asked.

♪✱

They didn't say a word to each other as they walked. But there was no need to say anything; they both knew they were heading toward the cemetery. The little one on the hill with eroding headstones so old they were slanting into the earth at odd angles. It was the place they'd first kissed. Where they'd made snow angels. Where he'd read to her from William Blake, e. e. cummings, and his favorite, Charles Bukowski. And on days when he was feeling brave, he'd lay her head in his lap and read to her from his notebook. He wished he had a poem for her right now about why she shouldn't leave him.

The sky had clouded over into a Rothko-esque slate-blue color field, saturating the graveyard with prestorm hues: the green of the grass, the white of the birch trunks, the yellow of the dandelions. As Anabelle and Matt silently climbed the hill, he picked a dandelion bouquet for her, and when they reached the top, he presented the flowering weeds to her with both hands, in the same pose as the sculpture he'd made on her jewelry box. He hoped she'd get the reference.

As she took the dandelions, she gave a knowing smile. A sad smile, but knowing nonetheless.

They sat down on their favorite bench in the shade of a

few trees, their papery bark peeling like pencil shavings. Thunder grumbled in the distance.

"I don't know what to say," Anabelle said, tying the stem of one dandelion around the head of another.

"We don't have to end this," Matt told her. "We can make it work."

"How, Matt?" She added another flower to the chain. "How will we make it work when we're in different states?"

"We won't see each other as much as we do now, but we'll visit."

"I'll probably have lots of homework. It'll be hard."

"I can drive out and see you. It's only like ten hours or something."

"But I might have so much work that I won't be able to spend much time with you. And then you'll feel bad." Anabelle tightened the knot on the next stem, and in the process popped the head off the last dandelion. "And you'll take it out on me."

She was making him feel like such a monster. Didn't she get that his anger over not showing him enough appreciation, his jealousy over Jonah, was all about how deeply he loved her? Wasn't that obvious? "I just wanted to prove that people can do it," he said.

"Do what?"

"That they can stay together. That they can be high school sweethearts and stay together. I just thought, if you're devoted enough, if you never stop showing each other that you're totally, completely in love, you can get through anything."

Anabelle held the dandelion chain up to her head. Her brow was all wrinkled and Matt wasn't sure if it was because she was trying to figure out if the chain was long enough, or because she was concentrating on what he'd just said. "You really think your parents could've worked it out?" she asked him.

"Well, not once my dad cheated. But before that. They could've stopped everything from going so wrong. If my mom hadn't been such a flirt. If my dad had paid her more attention in the first place."

"Maybe, sometimes, people shouldn't have ever been together." Anabelle carefully tied one last flower onto the chain and joined the two ends, completing the loop. "And maybe it's better to recognize it early, before you're married and have kids and it's too late."

"But we can do it. We can, I know we can. We care about each other."

Anabelle rubbed the top of one of the dandelions with her thumb.

"What're you thinking?" Matt asked.

"You said we care about each other."

"Yeah . . ."

"But you never seem to think I care about you."

"No, I do. Of course I do. I just get frustrated sometimes because I feel like I'm putting in more effort. Making you stuff, buying you stuff. But you're the most caring person I know."

There was another thunder roll, this time much closer. Anabelle gazed off into the direction of the impending storm. She had this look on her face as if she wasn't buying a word Matt was saying. As if it were impossible for her to believe that he actually thought she was caring.

"You *are*," he said. "I first fell for you because of your kindness. That night when I was wasted and you brought the trash basket to my bed and sat with me while I puked? Nobody else would've done that for me. Maybe Jonah. But it's not like I'd ever want to date Jonah. I'm just saying, no other girl has ever been so sweet to me. You used to do stuff like that all the time. You used to play me jazzy lullabies when I was sad. But then at some point you stopped. And I guess I felt abandoned."

A lightning bolt flashed in the baseball field across the

street. The thin crackly line looked unreal, as if it had been drawn in a comic book.

"I'm sorry," Anabelle told him, placing the dandelion crown over her bouncy ringlets. "I don't know what to say. I guess I care about you, but I don't want to always have to take care of you." She looked like a princess. Some kind of earthy goddess.

Matt's throat started to burn. It was a feeling he'd gotten used to during his parents' divorce—it came from swallowing his tears before they could leak out of his eyes. "I'd take care of you," he said, trying to control the quake in his voice. "Whatever you needed. Whenever you needed it."

"But I don't know if I'm ready to make that kind of commitment to you. And I'm not sure I want you to make it to me either." She said it completely calmly and stony-faced.

It was clear: she didn't *want* to make this work. She'd made up her mind, and if he kept trying to convince her that there was a solution, he'd just sound whiny. And yet, he couldn't help but whine. "What about us getting married?" he asked. They'd been planning on doing it right here at the little chapel in the cemetery the summer after she graduated Oberlin. A small wedding, only them and their families.

Anabelle just looked at him. Serene, elegant, and poised, like a sixteenth-century marble sculpture.

And then, he couldn't help it: in one big exhale, the tears let loose. It was as if a dam had broken behind his eyes. "What about Mount Desert Island? I've got the cabin booked." His voice sounded like some half-feminine version of himself.

"We should cancel it," she said simply.

He lifted the neck of his shirt and wiped his eyes as the thunder kaboomed straight overhead. "You know, I've actually been thinking we should break up," he lied. "For kind of a long time."

"Really?" she said, cocking her dandelion-crowned head.

"Uh-huh."

"Why?"

"Because," he said, "you make me too happy. And I can't create when I'm happy. No artist can."

"Oh," she said, sucking in her lower lip. "Well, I wouldn't want to hold you back."

There was something about seeing her hurt that made him able to stop crying so much. As if now they were even.

A few tiny raindrops fell on the grass in front of them. And then, within seconds, the sky completely opened up.

It was the kind of rain that made it impossible to see anything more than five feet away. But on their bench under the trees, all they felt was a little mist.

Matt leaned over and picked a dandelion from the grass. One of those fluffy ones that looked like a tiny globe of snow. He handed it to Anabelle. "Make a wish," he said.

She shut her eyes and held the dandelion under her chin. The rain whished. She blew.

The white airy seeds parachuted out into the storm.

Anabelle reached over to his eyelashes. "Hang on, one didn't make it." She pulled the seed off of his face and blew it away.

Then she picked a dandelion for him. "Your turn," she said.

Make this a good one, Matt told himself as he closed his eyes. He sat there for a second, letting the seeds tickle his lips. *I wish that we get back together someday,* he thought, huffing at the flower as if it were a birthday candle. There was something really romantic about the idea that this wasn't it, that they'd suffer for a while without one another and then realize that they just couldn't bear to live apart. Like Diego Rivera and Frida Kahlo.

"So this is really happening?" Anabelle asked.

"It's what you want, isn't it?"

"I guess. But it's so hard."

Matt grabbed her hand and squeezed it three times. Once for *I*, once for *love*, once for *you*. She waited a beat, then did the same back to him.

She leaned in close. "Can I, um . . . can I kiss you one last time?"

He answered her by pressing his lips to hers. It lasted through the next three rolls of thunder. The rain pounded down harder, creating a curtain all around them.

Matt ran his fingers along the bottom of Anabelle's belly. It was warm and soft. "Can I do this one last time?" he asked, creeping his hand up higher and higher under her shirt.

She nodded, pushing her hand inside the elastic of his boxers. "Can I do this one last time?"

"Uh-huh."

They weren't really *doing* anything, just holding each other in places where nobody else had ever touched them.

"I can't imagine doing stuff with anyone else," she said.

"I know, me neither," he said.

"Can we just sit here for a while?" she asked.

"Yes," he said. It's not like they could go anywhere else right now without getting soaked.

Matt looked out at the headstones, darkened from the

rain. There were the couples, the families. And then there were a few sad ones all off on their lonesome, their names worn off.

Anabelle leaned her head on his shoulder, her hair brushing the underside of his chin.

He was already imagining the poetry he could write about this moment, the paintings he could make. The sculptures. It was going to be a busy year.

{ **CHIN** *Deep* }

mary-tyler singletary

For the twenty-fifth day in a row, Mary-Tyler woke up imagining she was in a coffin.

Tucked tightly in her sheets, she lay on her back, listening—and heard absolutely nothing. Her eyes fluttered open and she saw the same pitch black as when they'd been shut. It could've been five A.M. or two in the afternoon; she didn't know and she didn't care. That was the freedom of being in a lightless room.

She could never keep it up for too long, though, because eventually she'd convince herself that she really *was* trapped in a box deep in the earth and there were all sorts of things up there in the living world that she'd miss: swinging on a rope over a stream; flipping on a trampoline; going on that salt 'n' pepper shaker ride at the little amusement park with the funny name. She *had* to get on that thing before her life was over.

Mary-Tyler took out her earplugs. And there was her dad's voice, somewhere outside the blackness: *Get a whiff of that honeysuckle! Is that to die for or what?* Then, the crisp snipping sounds of garden shears. She stood up and felt her way along her bed, and then the wall, until she reached her closet. She opened the closet door and groped around the inside, running her fingertips over a panel of buttons, and pushed the top one. The automated blinds whirred, first letting in pinpricks of light, then long stripes. Mary-Tyler squinted as the sun flooded her room and watched the blinds rise to the top of her two expansive windows—one on either side of the corner.

Down by the path to the beach was her father, all pudgy and balding and sucking on his water bottle with the little nipply top. As usual, he was standing beneath the garden-ers' ladders, pretending he wanted to make small talk but really making sure they didn't miss any spots—that they got the giraffes' necks just right.

Mary-Tyler groaned. She'd asked her father several times to let the gardeners do their work in peace. Last week she'd even made him a Bloody Mary—his favorite drink— and set it on a table by the pool, along with the *Wall Street Journal*, which she'd opened to the stock pages. But he'd just picked up the drink and the paper and carried them with him as he trailed the gardeners, eyeing their work while they shaped the elephants' tusks and the monkeys' tails; it was the thin, delicate parts he worried about most.

Once her eyes had adjusted to the light, Mary-Tyler threw on her fluffy white bathrobe to protect her legs from the arctic-cold air-conditioning and walked down to the second-floor bathroom, her flip-flops clapping against her soles. She undressed, trying not to catch a glimpse of herself in the mirror-lined walls and ceiling. It was impossible, though, to avoid seeing her body in reflection upon reflection upon reflection. She grabbed a handful of her stomach, wishing she could squeeze the blubber right out of it and—*presto!*—she'd be thin. Standing in the whirlpool tub, she turned the showerhead to its highest pressure setting and let it pelt water at her scalp like a barrage of BBs.

As she lathered up, she eyed her razor. She hadn't shaved her entire time here. It's not like there was a point; she didn't see anyone besides her parents. But maybe, she thought, just maybe if she did it today, it would give her motivation to venture away from this place, to be seen in public. She squirted a glob of pink shaving gel in her palm, then rubbed it into a foam over her armpits and legs and slowly scraped it off. After she'd rinsed and shut off the water, she felt a sharp stinging in both of her Achilles tendons. She knelt down to find blood trickling down her heels. Blade must've been too sharp. Or too dull, maybe.

She stepped out onto the floor and dragged her feet along the tiles, tracking trails of blood behind her—and in the never-ending reflections. She wondered what would happen if she'd cut her wrists instead of her heels.

How long would it take for her parents to realize she was lying in the tub bleeding?

♪❋

Mary-Tyler headed down the hall in one of her many black bathing suits—an athletic racer-back-type thing, to keep all her stuff tucked in neatly. Though, again, why did it matter if only her parents ever saw her? *One of these days,* she thought, *I should buy a two-piece.* Nothing too risqué—a tankini or something. Maybe she'd do it today, even, to go with her freshly shaven armpits and legs.

She walked down the spiral staircase, and when she got to the first-floor landing, she stopped and checked the thermostat. Sixty-eight degrees. Way too cold. She turned it up to seventy-five. No, seventy-six. Why did it need to be so cold in here when her parents spent all day outside anyway?

She punched the warming button up one more degree, then continued through what her mom called the "sitting room," the "den," and the "sunroom" until she reached the kitchen. There, she opened the fridge and found a plate wrapped in tinfoil, topped with a Post-it with her name on it. She lifted the foil. Today it was blueberry pancakes with bacon. Plus a glass of freshly squeezed juice, which sat beside the plate. When they were at the "cottage," Mary-Tyler's dad was in a constant state of squeezing oranges. That is, when he wasn't keeping an eye on the workers.

Being in the kitchen always put Mary-Tyler on edge. There were just too many things in there that she imagined could be used to damage herself. Obviously, there were knives, which she could use to chop off her hands.

But then there were other things, like boiling water or hot coffee, which she could dump all over her bare feet. Or the vegetable peeler, which could scoop out her eyes.

Trying not to look at the fancy gigantic corkscrew on the counter, she grabbed her breakfast, plus a bottle of pure maple syrup, and brought them out to the patio table.

The gardeners' snipping had fallen into a pattern of threes, echoing the call-and-response of the birds around them. There would be a *snip-snip-snip* from one, then a *snip-snip-snip* from the other—a waltz over the drone of a distant lawn mower.

Mary-Tyler poured herself a puddle of syrup, then plunged a strip of bacon into it and bit off an end. Cold, but still crisp. Just how she liked it.

"No, see there have to be two of each," she heard her dad say up ahead of her, somewhere inside the topiary. "Otherwise they can't reproduce."

"But it's bushes, man!" one gardener said. "Bushes can't do the reproduce!"

"Theoretically, I mean," her dad said sternly.

More snipping sounds.

"It makes perfect sense!" she heard her dad say. "Haven't

you ever read the story?! If we get flooded, we're all set!" He chuckled.

No laughter from the gardeners.

Mary-Tyler burst a berry against the roof of her mouth.

"Make sure one's a male and one's a female," her dad said. "Because obviously, that's the only way it'll work. Got it?"

He emerged from behind a rhinoceros and shook his head disapprovingly at a row of tree-shaped bushes, which he'd been going on about nonstop last night at dinner.

"They look too . . . lollipop-ish," he'd said.

Of course, Mary-Tyler had to pipe up and inform him that that wasn't even a word.

"Too much like a lollipop," he'd clarified.

"I know what you meant," she'd snapped. "But I just don't get it."

"Get what?"

"Why you have to make a tree look like a different kind of tree."

"It's not a tree to begin with," he'd told her, with the tone of a scolding teacher. "It's a bush."

Tree, bush. Same difference. Whatever words you wanted to use, it was still ridiculous. Beyond ridiculous.

♪✵

After breakfast—brunch? brinner?—Mary-Tyler spurted sunscreen on her limbs and rubbed it in until it stopped looking cream-cheesy.

She continued with her daily routine and walked across the lawn toward the pool. On her way, she saw something shiny glinting in the sun, hanging on the butt of one of the topiary bears. It had been pretty stormy recently and rain often churned up trash in their yard—yet another thing that really got her dad going. This piece of debris turned out to be a tangled mess of brown cassette tape. She always wondered how tape wound up on the streets in the city and had no idea how it could've landed in their yard. Were people in the habit of unraveling their tapes once they broke? And who even listened to cassettes anymore? She left it there, knowing her dad would find it and get pissed off—though hopefully not at the gardeners.

Her mother was in her usual spot by the pool's edge, sunning her perfectly thin self on a chaise lounge. Mary-Tyler wasn't sure what good it did her mom to get any more tan; she seemed to have hit her maximum browning potential at least a week ago. Didn't she get bored of lying around, doing nothing?

Mary-Tyler kicked off her flip-flops and stuck her toe in the water. Just a little cooler than air temperature. Nice.

The pool was designed to look "natural." "More like naturally *man-made*," Mary-Tyler had corrected her dad when he'd explained the concept to her. She couldn't imagine where in the natural environment you would find a small body of water surrounded by smooth slate, rocks jutting out around the perimeter as seats, and tiny cascading waterfalls punctuating the surface. And the diving board? How was *that* supposed to be natural? She was still waiting for an answer.

He'd been a jerk to the pool installation guys, too, lecturing about how the water should be greenish blue, not bluish green. Everyone who'd ever worked on the house hated them, and it was all her dad's fault. Why couldn't he see that?

Mary-Tyler descended down the pool steps, into the glassy *greenish-blue* water. She walked out a few paces, then got on her back and floated—arms to the sides, feet straight ahead, stomach flat.

She felt her chin-length hair spreading around her head, her ears underwater. She couldn't hear her dad, couldn't hear the workers. She couldn't even see them from where she was. All she saw was sky and wiggling tips of willow trees—a slow silent film moving to the sound track of the hollow gurgling beneath the surface of the pool.

On most days, she would look up at the clouds, searching for humanlike forms that she could build out of clay in her studio back at home. There was one formation she'd seen a few days ago that she'd already planned on replicating: a bunch of bodies all heaped on top of one another, and then right beside them one figure curled in on itself.

But today there were no clouds. Just clear, flat blue.

She felt her legs sinking and gave a little frog kick to keep herself afloat. Up above, a parasailer glided by, and she imagined what she must look like from a bird's-eye view. Lone girl stretched out in a "natural-looking" pool. Around her, a bright green lawn. Weirdo animal bushes. Lollipop-ish tree bushes. And then, off to the side, the ocean, the beach, and loads of people out enjoying the weather. Having fun, making friends, going on adventures. Her entire body filled with envy. She wanted to be out there doing whatever they were doing.

She wondered if maybe tonight "the vandals" would come back. That was her dad's name for those kids who'd snuck into their pool. Her dad was convinced they were the same people responsible for the rock that had gone through the workout-room window early in the summer. Mary-Tyler didn't believe they would've done that. They were just kids being kids. Kids having a good time. Ever since that night they'd shown up, she'd been staying up waiting for them, hoping that this time they wouldn't run away. Or that they'd take her with them. She'd hung on to the bowling shoes one of them had left behind; they fit perfectly on her ogre-size feet.

Mary-Tyler let herself sink underwater. Lately, she'd been timing herself to see how long she could hold her breath.

But today she didn't count. She just blew bubbles out of her nose, wondering how long it would take before she drowned, wondering if she'd even notice it happening. She imagined her parents' reactions if they found her dead in the pool. Would they realize that this wasn't an accident? That she'd done it to show them how much they were suffocating her?

No, Mary-Tyler thought. *They'd just add it to the list of things I've done to hurt them.* It would come right after getting a B in chemistry and before not entering a sculpture in the citywide high school art competition. Actually, it might top briefly dating the scholarship kid freshman year—the one who lived in Harlem.

I have to do something, she told herself. *I can't just keep waiting for fun to come to me. I have to go out and find it myself.*

Besides, she had smooth legs today, dammit.

♪✽

Mary-Tyler burst out of the pool, wrapped a towel around her waist, and ran toward the dirt path on the lawn, weaving between the oversize animals.

"Where're you off to in such a hurry?" her dad asked when she passed him. The nipple on his water bottle squeaked as he pulled it from his lips.

"Meeting a friend!" Mary-Tyler said. "I'm late!"

"I didn't know you knew anyone here!"

"It's someone from school who's in town! She just called! We're going shopping for back-to-school clothes!"

"In a *towel?*"

"Yeah," Mary Tyler shouted behind her, "just window shopping—on the boardwalk!" She ran down the wooden steps to her family's private beach, which nobody ever used except her.

She didn't know where she was going, except that she wanted to find some people. People who didn't sit around at their house all day. People who did things you were supposed to do on vacation: play tennis, volleyball, Frisbee. Blast a boom box while eating sandwiches from a cooler.

Maybe she'd even find Tobin, the only kid she'd ever met in this town. Then again, he'd been pretty skittish when he'd helped his dad install the pool, so maybe he didn't like her anyway. Probably because she was some annoying rich guy's daughter.

She turned left and jogged along the shore, past the house with plastic flamingos all over the lawn, past the house with the heart-shaped pool, past all of the other "cottages" and their private beaches, strung with hand-painted NO TRESPASSING signs.

♪✳

When she finally reached the public beach, people were doing exactly what she'd imagined. Building sandcastles, collecting shells, laughing under striped umbrellas. Everything was so lively. There was a circle of high school kids kicking around a Hacky Sack; she wished she knew how to play.

She kept going. Seagulls picked at old peanut butter and jelly sandwiches and bees buzzed around spilled sodas. Squealing children ran up to the edge of the water and then back as the surf chased them toward dry sand. She went past festive-looking families and kissing couples; groups of pimply preteens; twentysomething girls on their stomachs with untied bikini tops.

Nobody was there alone.

As she got closer to the jetty at the end of the beach, the groups started to thin out and blankets got farther and farther apart, until it was just sand between her and the rocks.

Then, off in the distance, something caught her eye. It sat a few feet back from the point in the sand where it went from lumpy and horizontal to flat and slanting toward the water. The thing looked like a head—a decapitated head—lying amid the dried seaweed and broken shells. She ran toward it, but as she got closer she slowed down. What if it really *was* a decapitated head? She wasn't sure she would know how to deal with that. Maybe she should leave it for someone else to find. But now she could see that the head belonged to a girl. A girl, probably about her age, with amazingly curly light brown hair that glinted in the sun. Mary-Tyler decided she'd better check it out; if *her* head had been cut off, she wouldn't want someone to let it sit there and rot.

She took a deep breath and got within a couple feet of the head. No blood. It didn't smell or anything. She squatted beside it. The glazed-over eyes were looking at the water, the lips pursed thoughtfully. She was trying to decide whether or not to touch the halo of ringlets when suddenly the head turned to face her. *"What?!"* it said, with a dirty look.

Mary-Tyler jumped backward and landed on her butt. "Jesus, I thought you were a head!" she said, out of breath. "Like, without a body!" *Wait, careful,* she thought. *Is that a handicap people can have?* "Do you *have* a body?" she asked, less delicately than she knew she should've. "I mean, you're not just a head, right?"

"Of course I have a body," the head said, and went back to looking at the water.

"Right, duh," Mary-Tyler said, smacking her forehead. She looked at the clumps of sand in front of the head and tried to imagine how far it was to her toes. Maybe she was extremely tall—like seven feet; it was impossible to tell. "That looks rad," Mary-Tyler said. "Mind if I join you?"

"I guess not," the head said uncertainly.

Mary-Tyler tossed off her towel and began to dig herself a pit. The sand on top was smooth and fine, like flour. A few inches down it became moist. She savored the clumps of cool, muddy wet grains between her fingers, and neatly piled them in walls around the body-size rectangular hole.

She packed down the sand on the bottom and the sides, picking out stray rocks, crab claws, and pieces of sea glass. *It would be fun to make a person out of sand,* she thought, and imagined sculpting a giant hand, a torso, a row of toes.

"Don't take this the wrong way," the head said, eyeing the hole. "But I think you'll need it wider than that."

Mary-Tyler looked down at her body. Even in her modest bathing suit, she still felt like she was spilling out everywhere, all cleavage and thighs. She quickly dug around the edges of the hole, anxious to cover herself under the sand.

"And longer," the head added. "You're kind of tall."

Mary-Tyler lay down beside the hole and saw that it came only to her ankles. "Good call," she said, and expanded the end a little past the point in the sand where it started to slant downward.

"And you'll want a pillow for your head," the head said.

"Oh! Thanks, good idea." Mary-Tyler built up a higher wall at the top of the hole. She climbed in to test it out. She mushed her body into the sand, making it fit her contours. "Maybe a little deeper," she said.

No reply from the head.

Mary-Tyler dug out a couple more inches of sand, then got in again. That seemed about right. She sat up and gathered the displaced sand over her feet, then her legs, and packed it in firmly. Then she lowered herself back down and covered her torso and shoulders.

"This is the tricky part," the head said. "The arms."

"I was just realizing that," Mary-Tyler said.

"You can bury one. But then you kind of have to make a pile up above your other elbow, then shove your hand in."

"Rad!" Mary-Tyler said. The technique worked perfectly.

"I just saved you a lot of time," the head said.

"I know. It's a good trick." Mary-Tyler looked out over where her body should be and saw nothing but sand. She felt cozy. As if she were being hugged by the earth.

A little bird—a sandpiper was it called?—hopped over their nonexistent bodies. Waves whished up ahead, at the bottom of the slope.

Mary-Tyler took a deep breath, catching a whiff of her sunscreen. "So, what's your name?" she asked.

"Anabelle," the head said hesitantly.

"Mine's Mary-Tyler."

Anabelle studied Mary-Tyler's face as if sizing her up.

Mary-Tyler looked back at the clusters of people on the other part of the beach. "Maybe this was a mistake," she said. "You don't seem to want me here." Even though it was late in the afternoon, the sun beat down on Mary-Tyler's face and she actually wished she'd brought that big straw sun hat her father was always bugging her to wear.

"Look, I don't want to seem rude, Mary," Anabelle said. "It's just, well, if you lived in Normal, you'd understand."

"It's, um, Mary-Tyler. That's my first name." She felt apologetic every time she had to correct people.

"That's unusual."

"Yeah." Mary-Tyler almost lifted her hand out of the sand to hold it over her face—but she stopped herself; she didn't want to ruin the illusion of decapitation. "It's this weird family thing. All the girls are named Mary-hyphen-their-dad's-name."

"So your dad's name is . . ."

"Tyler."

"And your mom?"

"Mary-Milton. And my grandma's Mary-Hank."

"Whoa. *Really?*" Anabelle's voice perked up.

"Yup."

"What about the boys? Do they get special names, too?"

"Jack."

"Just Jack?"

"Yeah."

"*All* of them?"

"Right. And then there's Aunt Jack. But I don't really know how that happened."

Anabelle laughed, shaking her head. "That just made my day," she said.

"What do you mean?"

"I like absurdity," Anabelle said. "And this name thing is pretty absurd. You have to admit."

"Yeah, I guess it is." Mary-Tyler half wanted to get out of her hole and walk away, but then where would she go? Home? "Hey, what were you saying before—about how I'd understand if I lived here?" she asked.

Anabelle turned to look at her. Her face was sunburned. Not everywhere, but on the tops of her forehead, nose, and cheeks—all the planes that faced upward. "Just that you'd understand how we feel about tourists, if you had to deal with them coming in every summer. And especially now, with McMansionville growing. Those people come into Taffy Castle all the time—where I work? And I want to strangle every one of them. They bring their bratty little kids with names like Mercedes and yell at me for being out of peanut brittle, when really we're a *taffy* shop and there's nothing in the name of the store that says we should have anything but taffy!"

Mary-Tyler shuddered as she remembered her dad

complaining about not being able to find peanut brittle the other day. "What's McMansionville?" she asked, with the terrible feeling that Anabelle was talking about her street.

Anabelle gestured to the right with her head. "That's what we call those ginormous beach houses over there."

"Oh, those fucking things," Mary-Tyler said, trying to sound as disdainful as possible. "Yeah, they're awful. And hey, anyway, what makes you think I'm a tourist?"

"Well, first, I don't recognize you. Even if you were from Bay Beach or Surprise, I probably would've seen you around. And second, kids around here don't say *rad*." Anabelle flicked her head sideways. "But hey, I'm sorry if I was mean. Don't take it personally or anything."

"It's okay. I know how it is. You thought I was one of *them*." Mary-Tyler made a hoity-toity face. "And I don't blame you."

"Yeah. But it's also—" Anabelle cleared her throat. "Well, I'm in a bad mood."

"What about?"

"Life."

"Do you feel like talking about it?"

"I don't know. Probably not."

This was good: Anabelle had a problem. And Mary-Tyler was great at helping people talk through their problems. Back home, kids she didn't even know that well sought her out for advice. Actually, what she gave wasn't quite advice, just a lot of question-asking and agreeing, making people feel like they were right. In any case, her listening skills were going to come in handy now in befriending Anabelle. "Well," she said, "I'm leaving in a few days to go back to New York. So you can feel safe telling me whatever, y'know?"

Anabelle looked Mary-Tyler up and down, from forehead to chin. "I wouldn't even know where to begin." She tilted her head back, squashing her curls. "But I guess it's not really that complicated. It just feels that way. It feels like there's nobody else in the world going through what I'm going through right now. And at the same time it seems so insignificant in the grand scheme of things and I wish I could just get over it."

Come on, Mary-Tyler thought. *Give me something I can latch onto.* "You're being pretty vague," she said, looking out at the ocean. The tide had started creeping up the sandy slope.

"Okay, if you *really* want to know . . ." Anabelle exhaled hard through her mouth and a small wisp of sand flew out from under her chin. "There's this guy I liked. A lot. I'm not even sure why. He's totally not my type."

"Why not?" *There we go,* Mary-Tyler thought. *Now she's opening up.*

"I don't know," Anabelle said. "I guess just because he's such a badass. Maybe it's not so much that he's not someone I should like, but that I never thought he'd like *me.*"

Mary-Tyler could hear Anabelle's voice relaxing; she was pretty sure she was winning her over. "Did he?" she asked.

"Yeah. Yeah, I think so. Maybe, probably. It's so dumb. He used to high-five me when we passed each other in the hall at school and it made me feel so cool, y'know? 'Cause he only did that with other guys. Then he started sitting on my lap all the time. Like in a joking way when we were hanging out in a group. And once he told me he had this dream. About me, like, floating over him and kissing him. I mean, what *is* that?"

"Are you kidding?" Mary-Tyler said, nodding at Anabelle. "It's him liking you. For sure."

"That's what I thought."

"But . . ." Mary-Tyler flattened her hand under the sand, indicating for Anabelle to continue, and then realized that Anabelle couldn't see it.

"But then, ugh—" Anabelle moaned. "This is where it starts to sound so stupid and petty. Like something out of a soap opera, you know?"

"Not really," Mary-Tyler said. "Give me specifics."

"Okay. Problem is . . ." Anabelle swallowed hard. "I had a boyfriend. A serious, long-term boyfriend. Not this badass guy I was telling you about. His, uh, best friend, actually."

"Uh-oh." Mary-Tyler was sure her scalp was burning, but she told herself to fight the temptation to get up.

Anabelle turned back toward the quickly approaching water. "You already think I'm awful. I can hear it in your voice."

"No, I'm not judging. I promise. I can just tell this is gonna get messy."

"Yeah," Anabelle said flatly. "It does."

No, no, no, don't shut down now, Mary Tyler thought. *You were just getting started!* "The boyfriend," she said encouragingly. "What's the deal with him?"

"Well," Anabelle continued cautiously, "he could kinda tell all along I had a thing for . . ."

"For Mr. Badass."

Anabelle let out a little laugh. "Yeah, so, my boyfriend was on my case about Sir Badass. And I swore up and down that he was wrong, that I wasn't dumping him for someone else." She tucked her chin and a few curls bounced forward, covering the side of her face. "The thing is, he was right.

I was dumping him for someone else. I had this stupid fantasy that I would run off with this guy and everything would be great."

Mary-Tyler was familiar with this feeling. "But it wasn't as amazing in real life as it seemed in your head?" she asked knowingly.

"Actually, it didn't get that far. We never even kissed or anything."

"Why not?"

"It's complicated."

"No, it's really simple. You obviously both want each other. And it's not like you'd be cheating or anything. You already broke up with your boyfriend. Who cares what you told him when you were together?"

"Well, the thing is, I could've kissed him. I could've kissed him after the breakup. I probably could've kissed him before the breakup. Trust me, I thought about it tons of times. Every time we were alone."

"So why didn't you? Why don't you get your butt out of this hole and go find him and just smooch him already?"

"I know, it's weird, right? When I'm away from him, all I can do is think about him. I'll run over and over in my head the sweet things he's said to me, the times he's touched me. But then when it seems like a chance comes up for something to really happen, I'm the one who stops it. I'll just start talking a mile a minute or laughing or something. And it seems crazy, y'know? Because I've been obsessing over him for months. But I just can't get myself to go through with it. Maybe it's because I've started noticing he's not perfect. Like how he smacks his lips when he eats. Or that he's got warts on his hands. Stuff that just snuck by me before."

"Funny how that can happen." This was exactly why Mary-Tyler's relationships never worked out. If you could even call them relationships; none of them ever lasted more than a month. There was always *something* that got under her skin.

"But that all seems so superficial, and that's not me."

Mary-Tyler knew what she meant. For her, those little things always seemed to be warning signs pointing to a bigger problem. "Well, maybe there's more to it than that," she said.

"Yeah, maybe. I guess there is something else. Something that's been bothering me about him, but it makes me feel bad to admit."

"What's that?"

"Well, last night we were talking about the future and stuff. And I just . . . I realized he's really never going anywhere. I mean, I knew he was planning on staying here, going to Normal Community, living with his mom, working the same job he's had the last couple years over at the bike shop. I knew all that. But somehow I'd convinced myself it was just temporary. That he wanted more." The sand above her chest rose and fell. "It's just so depressing," she said, getting a little teary. "He's got big dreams. Big ideas about things that nobody else I know ever thinks about. But he's never going to do anything about them. I just imagine myself coming home from college and I would've changed so much and he'd be exactly the same."

"Ooh, I know exactly what you mean. He's like those guys who are the epitome of cool until they start showing up at high school parties after they graduate."

"Exactly!" Anabelle said, cry-laughing. "He is totally going to turn into that guy." Her eyelashes were wet and clumped together as if she were wearing mascara. "But it's really bumming me out. Because now I'm feeling like I broke up with my boyfriend for nothing." Her voice sounded like it had been flattened under a house. Like it was the Wicked Witch of the East.

"Well, shit, that sucks," Mary-Tyler said, trying hard to fight back her envy. It was clear Anabelle had had something special with this boyfriend of hers. She'd found something that Mary-Tyler longed for but never experienced, something that she wasn't even sure was possible between two people. *This is about Anabelle,* she reminded herself, *not you.* "Do you want to talk about it more?" she asked. "Or be distracted?" This was Mary-Tyler's standard question when people told her their problems.

"Um, distract me," Anabelle said, sounding pleasantly surprised to have that as an option.

Okay, now she had to think of something. Something to make herself sound appealing. And definitely not rich. Mary-Tyler was drawing a blank. *Just say the first thing that comes to your mind,* she thought.

The waves roared, then crashed and sizzled just inches from where Mary-Tyler figured her feet were. She imagined each wave as a hand grasping at her body, trying to drag her out to sea. Right now they were still too far away to reach her, but not for long. Anabelle would be dragged off, too. It was kind of a romantic idea—two sad girls disappearing mysteriously into the sad, sad sea.

Jeez, snap out of it, Mary-Tyler told herself. There was no need to suck this innocent girl into one of her screwed-up death fantasies.

Mary-Tyler shut her eyes. She tried to picture the shape her body was making in the sand and wondered if there would be a way to make a cast of herself like this some-time—maybe in plaster?—like with the ruins at Pompeii. There, that was it. "You know what this reminds me of?" she asked Anabelle.

"What?"

"Have you ever seen pictures of the people who died by Mount Vesuvius?"

"You mean those people who turned to stone or some-thing?"

"Yeah, kinda," Mary-Tyler said. "They were buried in ash from a volcano and over time the ash hollowed out in the shapes of their bodies. And then, like sixteen, seven-teen centuries?—a hell of a long time later—this guy came up with an idea to fill in the empty spaces with plaster. So now you can see them in the positions that they were buried in."

"Oh. Yeah, I know what you're talking about. That's pretty creepy."

"But it's also really beautiful. They're, like, the perfect sculptures."

"Are you into sculpture?" Anabelle asked with a sidelong glance. She sounded disgusted, as if Mary-Tyler had just told her she liked to eat cockroaches.

"Yeah. It's what I spend most of my time doing back home. Why? You seem disappointed."

"It's just, well, my ex? He's an artist. Paints, writes poetry. And sculpts."

Great, Mary-Tyler thought. *You had to go and pick exactly the topic she didn't want to talk about.*

"This is kinda embarrassing. I'm not even sure why I'm telling you." Anabelle shrugged and her shoulder poked through the sand. "Anyway . . . I went to his house today. To, like, try to get back together."

"But he didn't want to?"

"You could say that. I found him building this clay bust of me. The mouth was stuffed, all gagged up with papers. Turns out they were hate poems he'd written for me."

"Asshole," Mary-Tyler said, guiltily satisfied. Anabelle hadn't found something special with this guy; she only thought she had.

"Yeah, I know. But it's my own fault. I should've never dumped him. Now I don't have him *or* the badass guy."

"Maybe it's not a choice between the two of them. Maybe

there's a third choice. Or a fourth or a fifth. Or maybe it's not about having a guy right now. Maybe it's just about having friends."

"Maybe. But in the middle of all this mess—I'm not sure how, exactly—I managed to lose my closest girl friend, too. I've got nobody."

"Hey!" Mary-Tyler said, sticking her neck out at Anabelle. "You have me!"

Anabelle turned toward Mary-Tyler, unconvinced. "We just met."

"How long does it take?"

"I don't know. But you're leaving in a few days, you said."

"So I guess we'll have to make the most of it."

Anabelle squinted. "Why do you want to be my friend so bad?"

"Because I'm sick of not having any friends here either, and you seem nice." Mary-Tyler remembered how Anabelle had snapped at her before. "Well, maybe *nice* isn't the right word. Interesting."

"I'll take interesting," Anabelle said, cracking a smile. "Most people would call me *nice* or *good*. I'm pretty tired of being thought of that way."

"Well, to me you're interesting."

"What's so interesting about me?"

"When I met you, you were just a head in the sand. You're still a head in the sand."

"That's true." Anabelle giggled. "You have no idea what I look like down there. I could have the body of a fish."

"You mean, like a mermaid?"

"No, an actual fish."

"That would be rad. I mean, *cool.* Or *groovy. Wicked.* Whatever the hell you locals say around here." Mary-Tyler pictured Anabelle's head on top of a mass of shimmery scales with fins and gills. "I guess there are no secrets with what I look like. You saw me get in. In all of my jiggling glory." As Mary-Tyler said it, she knew it was a weirdly aggressive thing to say. She hated when girls complained about their weight, and didn't like for other people to know she had body issues. *Please don't tell me I'm not fat,* she thought, bracing herself for Anabelle's response. *It'll just make me feel worse.*

Suddenly it felt as if someone had thrown ice cubes against Mary-Tyler's big toes. She looked up to see that the water had exposed them with their chipping black polish, like little sand creatures burrowing for food. She watched the waves lapping their way up the slope. How many more would it take for her whole body to feel encased in ice? Maybe just one big one.

Anabelle finally spoke. "Tell me more about those ash people," she said. "About how they're the perfect sculptures."

"Oh, right." Mary-Tyler was caught off guard, not only because Anabelle hadn't said anything about that weight comment but because she'd actually been paying attention. At school, kids basically saw Mary-Tyler as a receptacle for gut-spilling. They *never* asked her questions. Maybe this actually *was* the start of an honest-to-God friendship. "They're perfect sculptures," she explained to Anabelle, "because they're so natural. There's no stupid forced pose or facial expression. They're just *reacting*." Mary-Tyler tried not to wince as another freezing-cold wave encapsulated her foot. "I've always wondered what pose I'd be in if I were caught in a volcano."

"Or caught in the sand at the beach?" Anabelle gestured at their hidden bodies with her head.

"Yeah, well, that's what was making me think of it! Because if we could figure out a way of getting out of here without disrupting the sand, we'd have perfect molds of our bodies at this moment."

"Would that be *rad* or what?" Anabelle laughed. It was

a deep laugh, reaching way down past her vocal cords and into her chest. Way too deep for the small girl that suddenly came bursting out of her sand grave and jumped around in the foamy surf.

♪＊

The girls decided to get dinner over at the seafood shack on the boardwalk. Anabelle was the only one with money since she'd been wearing actual clothes with pockets, so she bought them a bag of lobster bodies—the cheapest thing on the menu. They sat across from each other at one of the patio picnic tables, watching as people packed up their beach gear over on the sand.

Mary-Tyler had no clue what to do with a lobster that was missing its claws and tail, but she tried to play it cool and pretend like she was a lobster aficionado. It didn't really matter, though. Anabelle wasn't paying one shred of attention to Mary-Tyler; her head seemed to be somewhere else entirely as she tore into her first lobster body. After cracking the thing in half, she started scooping out tiny bits of meat with her fingers. She looked like a predatory bird dismantling its prey. And she didn't even seem grossed out by the green stuff that was dripping onto her plate.

Mary-Tyler eyed her lobster bib and shell crackers, tools

she'd become accustomed to using when eating lobster. She didn't like the idea of breaking this creature's chest open with her bare hands—it felt a little like surgery. And not just surgery, but malpractice. But to use the crackers felt a little like eating with a fork at a Chinese restaurant.

Okay, she thought. *Just do it and get it over with.* She cupped the smooth bright orange body in her palms and lined her fingers up against the slit down the middle, just like Anabelle had, and gave it one big snap. Warm lobster juice ran down her wrists. She dropped the open body on her plate and stared at its insides, completely oblivious as to where to find sustenance in this thing.

Anabelle was picking off the legs methodically one at a time, giving them a single twist at their bottom joint. Mary-Tyler couldn't imagine doing that to her lobster; it looked too violent, like an ancient torture method or something. Yes, she knew the thing was dead. But still.

Anabelle finally broke out of her lobster-dismantling trance. "I've been doing something really bad," she said without looking up.

The statement startled Mary-Tyler. Anabelle had said it with such gravity that it made her wonder if Anabelle also fantasized about dying. "What do you mean?" she asked, realizing she was hoping Anabelle was suicidal, which was a really weird thing to hope about someone. Especially someone you liked.

Anabelle slowly sucked the meat out of one of her legs. "I can't talk about it."

"C'mon. No, you have to. You must've wanted to tell me if you brought it up."

"Sometimes when I think too much . . ." There was a clicking sound in Anabelle's throat and then a loud sigh. "I hurt myself," she whispered.

"Wait, what do you mean?" Mary-Tyler asked quietly.

"It's different at different times. But, like, today I was punching a brick wall."

Mary-Tyler looked at Anabelle's hands. Her knuckles were covered in tiny scrapes.

"Sometimes when there's nothing else to hit, I hit myself. I know, it's awful. But I get some sort of perverse pleasure out of doing it. Or, I don't know, it makes me feel worse. And somehow I actually *like* making myself feel worse. Sounds . . ." She looked up, as if searching for the right word. "Fucked up, doesn't it?"

"No, no, I get it," Mary-Tyler said. "I'm that way, too." Her heart pounded furiously with the knowledge that she was about to reveal a secret—about her disturbing thoughts, about the incident this morning in the pool.

"Really?"

"Totally. It's like you get to a certain degree of sadness and you just want to wallow in it. I've been doing the same kind of thing this whole vacation." *Wait a second,* Mary-Tyler thought, catching herself. *You can't tell her about the pool. She'd know where you live.*

"That's really nice of you to say, but I doubt it." Anabelle shook her head and her curls bounced vigorously. "For me it got so bad, I had to do something to myself physically to stop." She pointed toward the beach with a lobster leg. "And that's how I wound up there. I needed to put myself in the ground to keep from literally beating myself up. You can't tell me that's not bizarre."

Mary-Tyler brushed off some of the sand that was still stuck to her elbow. "Well, I got in, too, right?" she said, and left it at that.

Anabelle's face relaxed. "Yeah. I guess you did." She glanced at Mary-Tyler's lobster body. "Hey," she said, "you having trouble with that?"

"No," Mary-Tyler said quickly. "I was just taking a break—listening to you."

"Here, give it," Anabelle said, taking Mary-Tyler's plate. "I can do it fast. You're a tail-eater, it's okay."

"Tail eater? That doesn't sound like a nice thing to be."

"No, don't feel bad," Anabelle said. "It's just the truth. The parts that're chopped off of these things? Those go to the tourists. Us locals eat what's left. I think I've had a tail maybe twice in my life."

Mary-Tyler tried to imagine her parents picking apart a lobster like this. They always threw away the bodies when they ate whole lobsters. "Well, thanks for doing my dirty work for me," she said.

"No problem. I actually enjoy it. It's kinda like digging for treasure. The stuff is lodged in the cartilage in little shapes." Anabelle started piling bits of meat on the side of Mary-Tyler's plate. "Like your ash people."

Mary-Tyler grabbed a piece of lobster and put it in her mouth, rolling it around her tongue. It was really sweet and tender. Almost like tail meat. She couldn't wait to freak out her parents by eating straight from the chest the next time they got lobsters.

She pictured them right now munching in silence at their long dining-room table and realized she didn't want the day to end when she and Anabelle were through with their lobster bodies. "Hey, you doing anything after this?" she asked.

"No," Anabelle said. "I was just gonna go home. Maybe play piano for a few hours, keep my hands busy. Stop myself from turning into a psycho."

Mary-Tyler laughed. "How about *I* stop you from turning into a psycho."

"Okay," Anabelle said, pulling another body out of the bag. "What'll we do?"

"I'm in the mood for something fun. Something I've never done before," Mary-Tyler said. "Like, I've always wanted to go on that salt 'n' pepper shaker thingy. You know, at Twirly World."

"You mean *Whirrrly* World?"

"What*ever.*"

"Yeah, I don't know. Those kind of rides make me nauseous."

"Okay, let's stay away from there, then."

A seagull separated from his flock and paced back and forth alongside their table, waiting for them to drop bits of their food. Anabelle swung her legs at him and he backed up, but kept staring with beady mustard-yellow eyes. "You know, there *is* someplace I've been thinking about going," she said. "But it's sort of . . . I don't know, a naughty thing to do."

"Ooh," Mary-Tyler said. "What's the place?"

"Actually," Anabelle said, "maybe we shouldn't go there. You're gonna think I'm crazy."

"I'm gonna think you're crazier if you don't tell me already!"

"Okay." Anabelle shoved Mary-Tyler's lobster-filled plate back at her. "It's the nude beach?" she said, almost like a question.

"There's a *nude* beach here?!" Mary-Tyler said. "How can we *not* go?"

"Well, it's kinda far. Over at the bluffs."

"I don't mind."

"It doesn't weird you out?"

"I'm around nude people all the time back home. Sculpture classes."

"All right," Anabelle said, bobbing her head nervously. "That's what we'll do then. The nude beach."

Mary-Tyler twisted a leg off of her lobster carcass. "I can't believe you've lived here all your life and you've never been to the nude beach!"

"My boyfriend used to go," Anabelle said defensively.

"He never wanted me to go with him. I guess he didn't want me around when he was checking out girls."

Mary-Tyler was sure now: this guy had not been Anabelle's soul mate. Maybe Anabelle hadn't figured that out for herself yet. But she seemed like a smart girl; it was just a matter of time.

♪＊

The sun had dropped a bit since they'd left the beach, and its rays bathed the bluffs in a soft orange glow.

"Okay, ready?" Anabelle asked as they entered the small parking lot.

Mary-Tyler carefully rewrapped her towel around her waist, then gave an overly excited "Hell, yeah!" to not come off as prudish.

There were no nudists in the lot—only a few clothed people loading beach chairs and colorful bags into their trunks. Off to the side, at the edge of the bluffs, were two boys carrying binoculars, maybe twelve years old. Mary-Tyler wondered if the kids would be able to see them in their binoculars once they were down on the beach. But it didn't matter, right? It's not like she and Anabelle were gonna get naked or anything; they were just going to *look*.

They walked cautiously toward the stairs that led to the bottom of the bluffs. On the railing was a sign on a plank of wood:

NO NUDITY IN LOT/STAIRS
WAIT TILL ON BEACH!!!

"Darn, I thought I'd go down the steps naked," Anabelle said.

"Yeah," Mary-Tyler said. "Slide down the banister and get splinter ass!"

About every fifteen steps there was a landing and a ninety-degree turn. On their descent, they passed a young couple with a picnic basket and three balding guys with hairy backs. Mary-Tyler couldn't help but imagine all of them without their clothes on.

When they got to the bottom, they came across their first nudists. An elderly couple shaking sand out of their blanket. They wore only glasses, watches, and sandals. "Evening," the man said as he leaned over to pick up his newspaper. Even with dusk approaching, there was enough light to see his body clearly: wrinkly rear, silvery public hair, penis limply poking through the hair.

"Uh, hi," Anabelle said awkwardly.

"Okay," Mary-Tyler whispered when they'd passed the couple. "This is a little weirder than nude people in sculpting class! Did you see that woman's boobs? They were sagging so far, she could, like, pick her belly button with her nipples!"

"Shhhh!" Anabelle whispered, giggling. "That guy was a Polar Bear! I *really* didn't need to see him without his trunks."

"Polar bear?" Mary-Tyler said. "He looked human to me."

"No, the Polar Bear Club," Anabelle said. "It's a bunch of crazy old dudes who go swimming in the winter." Her face reddened. "Plus me."

"Wow, that's rad," Mary-Tyler said. "I don't think I'd have the balls to do that."

"Well, nobody knows I have the, uh, balls to do that," Anabelle confided shyly. "You're the only one I've told. I mean, I've only gone once, so it's not a huge deal, but if my friends had known, they would've turned it into one."

Wow, another secret. Mary-Tyler wanted desperately to return the show of confidence, to tell Anabelle that she wasn't as stable as she might seem. But how do you say to someone you just met, *I think about killing myself almost every second of the day*? It was way too heavy.

They continued down the ribbon of sand that wound around the bluffs, sticking close to the shore. The blankets were spread farther apart here than at the regular beach—but the nudies had all the same things as the clothed people: umbrellas, coolers, radios. And nobody was making any attempt to hide their bodies, no matter what shape they were in. A couple guys with beer guts lay around talking to women with belly-button piercings and tattoos as if nothing was out of the ordinary.

Anabelle stood on her toes and held a hand up to Mary-Tyler's ear. "We should've brought sunglasses," she said. "So we could look without looking like we're looking."

"Some of these people I don't want to be looking at anyway."

"Yeah, I know. I think I just passed my mailman."

"Eew," Mary-Tyler said. "See any hotties yet?"

"No," Anabelle said. "Okay, maybe one. But I'm starting to think guys are hotter *without* all their junk hanging out."

"Yeah, like that guy over there," Mary-Tyler said, trying to inconspicuously point at the guy in the shades leaning against the rocks, chatting up the tall, thin woman wearing only a visor. The guy's chest was so smooth, it looked like it had been waxed. And his pubic hair had *definitely* been waxed. "Nasty!" Mary-Tyler whispered, hunching over to Anabelle's ear. "Why would you shave your pubes?"

"Oh jeez," Anabelle said, tugging at Mary-Tyler's arm and picking up her pace. "That guy used to date my ex's mom! How come I know everyone here?"

Mary-Tyler snuck another look at the guy. There was something familiar about him, but she couldn't place what. And then, he caught her looking. He stopped talking to the visor woman and looked straight at Mary-Tyler. He lifted his sunglasses, and the way his eyes scanned her body, it was as if he could see right through her towel, her bathing suit. It was flattering and gross all at once. *Wait a minute,* she thought. *That's the pool guy!* Suddenly all of the flattery was gone and it was nothing but gross.

"Stop staring!" Anabelle whispered emphatically. "You have to be more subtle!"

"Sorry," Mary-Tyler said. "I thought I knew that guy from somewhere." *Remember,* she told herself, *don't let on that you have a pool.*

"Him?" Anabelle said. "I don't want to know how you know him."

"Why not?"

"He's, like, the town sleazeball. He struts around the

beach—the regular beach—in this little black Speedo. And he hits on pretty much everyone."

"Oh," Mary-Tyler said. "I guess that's why I recognized him. From the beach or something."

She turned around to see if the guy was still giving her that creepy look. Thankfully, he was back to Visor Woman. But a bunch of other people were watching her. "Hey," she said, tapping Anabelle's shoulder. "I'm getting this weird feeling. Like we don't belong here."

"Sorry. Was this a bad idea?"

"No, I'm just feeling like we're calling attention to ourselves because we're the only ones with clothes on."

"I know. I'm feeling the same thing," Anabelle said. "Like *we're* the ones revealing something about ourselves." She stopped in her tracks and turned on her heels. "Maybe we should change that?"

"What, take off our clothes? *Really?*"

"I don't know." Anabelle shifted her feet in the wet sand. "I mean, we must look like a couple of wusses. And maybe that's what I am. But I'm sick of being a wuss! You know what I mean?"

"Okay," Mary-Tyler said tentatively. Her skin tingled and tightened. "I'm in if you're in."

"Okay."

They stood there, staring at each other.

Then Anabelle turned her back to Mary-Tyler. She removed her shirt and shorts and, in a flash, her bra and underwear were off, too.

Mary-Tyler, realizing she was the *only* person left on the beach with clothes, turned her back to Anabelle and quickly threw her towel down and stripped off her bathing suit. She paused for a second, then turned back around and found that Anabelle was facing her already.

They both made awkward eye contact, clearly trying not to look below each other's chins.

"Okay, so, um, I guess we keep walking?" Mary-Tyler said, picking up her towel and suit. She kept telling herself to stop sneaking looks at Anabelle's body, which she now saw was much more elegant-looking, much more perfect and compact than it had appeared in her baggy clothes. Her back was pale and gleaming, with a couple wide strap marks framing her freckled shoulders where a tank top must've masked her skin from the sun.

Mary-Tyler bundled up her towel and suit in front of her chest. She felt as if her breasts were screaming out to the world, *Look at us! We're globes!* She had expected this to be easier; the models at the Sculpture Studio in New York sure made it look like it was nothing.

"You know," Anabelle said, not looking up at Mary-Tyler. "If we go in the water, we'll be covered up but still naked."

Mary-Tyler looked out at the ocean. It was vast, bottomless. The thought of going in there made her knees lock up. "Go ahead if you want," she told Anabelle.

"Can you swim?"

"Yeah, it's not that."

"What is it, then?"

"I don't . . . I don't know." She really didn't. All she knew was that the more she watched the water, the more the world around her was blending into a milk shake.

"Okay." Anabelle shrugged. "Well, feel free to join me if you want." She tossed her suit behind her and plowed into the water.

Mary-Tyler suddenly felt very alone and very naked. She really wanted to go in. So what was her problem?

As she watched Anabelle riding waves, the water rolled in over Mary-Tyler's feet, pulling them deeper and deeper into the sand. Seaweed swirled around her ankles and the undertow tugged at the backs of her legs, stinging the shaving cuts on her heels.

That was it: the undertow.

A memory flashed into Mary-Tyler's mind. A memory of being five years old at the beach. She'd separated from her parents, gone off to hang out at the shoreline by herself. There was a boy who looked like a young Luke Skywalker wading in up to his waist. She'd wanted to get a better look at him, so she'd walked into the water. She'd gotten out to where he was, and then—*bam!*—a wave smashed her over the head, toppling her over into an unplanned somersault. Her nose had filled with water. Her ears, her mouth. She was sure this was what it felt like to die.

And she hadn't gone in the ocean since. Not past her knees, anyway.

Imagining herself dying from her razor, from a kitchen tool, from the pool, felt totally different from potentially dying in the ocean. Out here, she'd have no control over how far the fantasy would go; she couldn't stop it like she had this morning in the pool. But she was going to die someday and maybe this was exactly the right way to go. On an adventure with her new friend.

She dropped her bathing suit and towel. And before she knew it, she was running. In slow motion. As if she were pedaling a bike uphill.

"Hey, you're in!" Anabelle shouted when Mary-Tyler made it up to her neck.

Water dripped over Mary-Tyler's lips and she licked it. It was salty. Saltier than sweat. Just the taste made her stomach tumble. "This is as far as I want to go, though," she said. "My feet can still touch the ground."

"Not for long," Anabelle said. A wave gently lifted Mary-Tyler's toes off the sand. The water was freezing cold and she could hear herself breathing inside her head.

"Relax," Anabelle said. "Let the waves carry you."

"It *is* sort of nice," Mary-Tyler admitted, her body buoyant from the thrill of doing something she thought might kill her. "Having the water touch you directly, you know? Feeling the waves pass over you."

"Yeah, they kinda tickle as they go," Anabelle said. "Totally different from being in here with a suit on."

Off past the buoys, Mary-Tyler saw a wave building. But it wasn't smooth like the other waves they'd been riding. This one was high with a frothing peak. And it was heading right toward them.

"I have to get out," Mary-Tyler said, feeling as if her body was made of bricks. "I can't go over that one. It's too much."

"You don't go over those," Anabelle said. "You go through them."

"*Through* them? That's even worse!"

"No, those are the best. They give you a huge rush."

"I can't," Mary-Tyler said. Her legs went stiff and she started sinking. She held her breath as her nose went underwater. This was it. It was over.

Then there was Anabelle's arm around her back, lifting her to the surface.

And the wave gathering speed.

And Anabelle saying, "Okay, on the count of three. Take a deep breath and dive through."

One . . . two . . .

And the gasping for a last breath of air.

. . . three.

Mary-Tyler ducked into the curling wall of water. Anabelle's hand was at the small of her back, guiding her through. The water yanked her backward, but she pushed on ahead, kicking her legs.

After a few seconds, the force subsided and her head popped out into the warm air. "We made it!" she shouted. Her heart was knocking on the inside of her chest, as if it were the police at a suspect's door.

"Of course we made it! I told you we would," Anabelle

said, her cheeks rosy and glistening with salt water. "See? I can be your sides of the pool to grab onto."

Mary-Tyler's throat felt raw, but in a good, alive sort of way. She couldn't stop laughing. It had been so long since she'd laughed, her laughter sounded like a foreign language.

"It seems like you liked it," Anabelle said.

"It was totally rad! My head's all spinny and like it's made of cotton candy!" Mary-Tyler's heart started to return to its normal pace, and for the first time since she got to this beach, she felt free to look all around her. Down at their bodies, distorting under the rippling water like a cubist painting. Back at the specks of people on even tinier specks of sand. Up at the darkening sky, sprayed with a smattering of just-starting-to-sparkle stars.

Anabelle pinched Mary-Tyler's arm hard. "Get ready, here comes another."

"Oh shit, you're right."

This time Mary-Tyler joined in with the counting. By the time they got to three, the wave was just about to crash over their heads.

Together they inhaled, closed their eyes, and dove through, headfirst.

{ The **VIEW** *from the* **TOP** }

anabelle seulliere

Anabelle's last night in Normal was an evening of *why nots.*

Why not have funnel cake, a soft pretzel, and a Sno-Kone for dinner; why not finally take on her dad's challenge with the strongman mallet, even though she knew she was going to lose; and why not go for one final ride with him on the Ferris wheel?

Well, this "final" ride would actually just be her second. The only other time she'd gone on the Ferris wheel was also with her dad. She was seven, and it had been a disaster. She'd actually really liked it until they'd hit the top, when she'd looked down and realized how far up they were. And after that, she'd turned into an ice sculpture, holding her breath for practically the entire rest of the ride. Ever since then, she hadn't had the guts to go on it—or any other rides that took you up high. Which basically left the Scrambler and Scat. Unless you counted kiddie rides like the carousel and the Tipsy Teacups.

But tomorrow she was going to college. Tomorrow she'd be a new person. So why not be a person who didn't freak out over stupid little things like going on the Ferris wheel. Right? Why not?

"I'm so proud of you for taking this risk, Annie," her dad said as the ride operator locked them into their basket. "But I guess I shouldn't be so surprised." He nudged her with one of his big bony elbows. "You've always been bold under that shy exterior. Anyone can see it, from how you tickle those ivories!" He ran his long spidery fingers up and down the front of their basket as if playing the piano.

The operator went back to the controls and their basket got pushed back one position, just above the heads of the people walking by.

"Da-ad," Anabelle moaned. It always embarrassed her
when he went on about her shyness. She hoped the operator hadn't been listening. "Just don't make a big deal out of
this, okay? Otherwise maybe I'll flip out *this* time, too."

But before she could even think about what it would be
like to rise any higher, there was a loud clanking sound
beneath them. Anabelle looked down and saw a guy shoving another guy up against the fence that surrounded the
Ferris wheel. And then the guy doing the shoving—the one
with the shiny black shirt unbuttoned halfway down his
exposed chest—punched the other guy.

It sounded like a rock hitting a beanbag, only with
something crunchy inside.

The guy who'd gotten punched cried out in pain and
looked up, holding his nose. There was something familiar about his face, but Anabelle wasn't sure if she knew
him. Then he let go of his nose, and even with the blood
gushing over his mouth and a freshly shaven head, Anabelle could tell: it was Jonah. He looked so weird without
any hair.

The exposed-chest guy—Anabelle now realized it was
creepy Steve, who used to date Matt's mom—grabbed Jonah
by his collar and yelled something Anabelle couldn't quite

make out. Something about Jonah fucking around with his woman?

Huh? What woman? Had Steve been doing it with a high school girl?

"Hey, cool it, Mack!" her father shouted down at Steve. He called all men whose names he didn't know Mack.

Anabelle shushed her dad. She just wanted the ride to continue and be over with, but the operator was frozen at the switch, watching the fight unfold.

The line for the Ferris wheel dispersed and a ring formed around Jonah and Steve. Behind the crowd, people were shooting darts at balloons, balls into baskets, and water guns at tiny round targets. Anabelle always found it strange to see grown men compete so vigorously at games, just to win hard stuffed animals for their dates.

Steve kept screaming obscenities, his wiry slicked-back hair shaking into his crimson face, while Jonah pinched his bloody nose and tilted his head toward the sky. "She came on to *me*, okay!" he yelled. "Did she ever tell you that part?" Who were they talking about? Anabelle ran through her head all of the girls she knew Jonah had dated. She couldn't imagine any of them sleeping with Steve. Not even that slutty college girl he'd had a one-night stand with last summer.

Maybe there was someone new. Someone Jonah had hooked up with in the last couple weeks since Anabelle had stopped hanging out with him. Even though it had been her decision not to pursue things, it made her sad to think he'd found someone else so quickly.

"What were you thinking?" Steve shouted. "Aren't there enough girls your own age?"

Jonah's own age? So this person was older? Anabelle remembered him saying something about needing advice from Jeanie about some mysterious older woman. Who could it be, though? Some girlfriend of Steve's? That didn't really narrow it down. He seemed to have a different one every time Anabelle saw him.

Steve stuck his face up in Jonah's and said something that was hard to make out. Something about finally finding love. Jonah fucking it all up.

"Wait, wait, wait, let go, okay?" Jonah pleaded. "Let me just explain."

Steve backed off a little but kept holding Jonah's collar.

"It was her idea, that's the truth. I told her we had to cool it, it wasn't going to work. And then she kept after me. Like, every time I was over there. What was I supposed to do?"

"Say no. Walk away. That's what." Steve reared his fist back as if getting ready to punch Jonah again.

Jonah winced. "I swear, I'm not gonna let it happen any—"

Just then, another guy came charging through the crowd and grabbed Steve by the shoulders. Anabelle couldn't hear what this new guy was saying, but from his tone she could tell it was vicious. This guy had curly hair—a boy version of hers—and it shook as he spoke to Steve. Hang on, she knew those shaking curls. They had to be Tobin Wood's.

She remembered suddenly that Tobin was Steve's son. It was hard for her to imagine that the two of them shared DNA; Tobin was so sweet and awkward. Plus, she never saw them in the same place at the same time because Steve never showed up for Tobin's concerts.

Steve yelled something unintelligible at Tobin and he backed off, surrendering with his hands in the air. Then he looked around as if he were lost at a fork in the road and couldn't figure out which direction to go. There was no line for the Ferris wheel, and he made his getaway through the entrance, dashing into the empty basket. The one right in front of Anabelle.

The ride operator ran up to the basket and Tobin handed him something—probably a ticket. Tobin's basket was the last one to be filled, and once he was set, the ride started inching backward.

"Wild Wild Life" was blasting on the WhirrrlyWorld speakers. They'd been playing the Talking Heads for three songs in a row, and Anabelle was glad: the Talking Heads always made her feel like dancing no matter what mood she was in. Even so, it was hard to trick herself into feeling happy. She was still stuck on trying to figure out who this older woman was.

Her mind was an ice-skater, racing 'round and 'round, just like Anabelle did out on Saco Pond every winter. She whizzed by different women's names—*no, too young . . . too old . . . not pretty enough*—until she stumbled upon one that seemed to fit all the criteria. This name was like that inevitable bump in the ice that would always trip Anabelle up; once she knew it was there, she'd avoid skating over it at all costs. But the quicker her head worked, the more frequently that name came up and she couldn't help slamming into it and careening out across the pond's black, slippery surface.

There was no getting around it: this was a person who had dated Steve. A person whose house Jonah went to all the time.

And this was a person who had discouraged Anabelle from pursuing Jonah. Maybe for more reasons than she had let on?

The basket rose and Anabelle focused on the top of

Tobin's head, forcing all Jonah-related thoughts from her mind. It was sort of thrilling to be able to see Tobin from this perspective—to watch him without him seeing her.

"That poor kid," her dad said loudly, because that was the only volume he spoke at. "To have a father like that. Such a shame."

"Dad," Anabelle scolded. "He'll hear you!" She wondered if Tobin *had* heard, but he didn't look up. Part of her wished he'd notice she was there, that he'd see she was wearing his red hoodie. The one he'd thrown at her that night of the *Cabaret* cast party. That night out on the trampoline, when he'd played her the slow movement of Schubert's Piano Trio in B-flat. She'd taken the recording out of the library and taught herself the piano part imagining that someday, if Tobin ever talked to her again, they could play the piece together.

The Ferris wheel had just passed the three-o'clock position—the point at which they switched from going backward to forward. Which meant there was now less than a quarter of the circle between them and the top. Anabelle gripped the side of the basket and told herself not to look down.

"That Wood kid," her dad whispered, pointing down at

Tobin. "He's leaving, too, right?" Even his whispers were loud.

Anabelle nodded.

"I can't believe a father would act like that at such an important time." He covered his extended index finger with his hand so only she could see that he was pointing down at Steve, who was still cursing like crazy despite the fact that Jonah had gotten away.

Anabelle put her finger to her lips. "Not everybody's father cares as much as you do," she said. The basket got higher and she lost sight of Tobin. He was starting to drift behind them.

"I know, I know. I just can't believe you're actually starting college," he said, his hand quickly tapping his chest, water pooling in the corners of his eyes—just how it always started.

"Promise me, no sobbing," Anabelle said, shrinking in her seat.

"Oh, Annie," her dad said, mid-sniffle, "I can't promise any such thing."

"Come on, you've had *eighteen years* to prepare for this," Anabelle said as they rose past the mast of the pirate ship. Its lights twinkled and swung under the star-studded sky.

"Eighteen years! Eighteen years?! Just *yesterday* I was taking you for a ride on the Teacups." He pulled off his glasses and wiped the tears away with the backs of his wrists. "The carousel!"

"Kiddie rides," she said. "And I'm not a kid."

He sighed and petted the back of her head. "Hey, how're you doing with this?" he asked, pointing toward the ground.

"Totally fine," Anabelle said overconfidently, as if trying to convince herself. *Right?* she thought. *It is totally fine.* To prove it, she looked down over the side of the basket. They were right about at two o'clock. Maybe two-thirty. Steve had finally wandered off, and a new line was forming for the Ferris wheel. *This really isn't so bad,* she thought, and stuck her neck farther out over the side.

Then she saw the floor of WhirrrlyWorld directly beneath them, and she suddenly felt like she did when she was seven years old. She whipped her head back to face forward, then pulled her legs into the basket and brought her hands up to either side of her face as blinders.

Waves of screams echoed from the roller coaster, the swings, the pirate ship. It sounded like everyone was having so much fun. She wished she could be feeling that way, too. Instead, her head was back out in the middle of the ice, spinning: *What kind of person hooks up with his best friend's mom? What kind of person am I to pine for someone like that?* Was there anyone out there who was right for her? Anyone at all? Or did everyone who seemed great at first turn out to have some fatal flaw?

"Earth to Annie!" her dad said, waving his hand in front of her face. "You there?"

"Yeah," she said, removing her blinders and looking straight at his long, jowly face. "I'm here." She didn't want to make him think she couldn't handle the ride—then he'd just start to panic.

"Well, we were having a conversation, remember?"

"Sorry," Anabelle said. "I zoned. What was the last thing you said?" Everything was okay, she told herself. All she had to do was fix her eyes on the dots of light reflecting in his glasses.

"I was talking about how it's not possible that you're going to college yet. How you're still our little baby!" His voice sounded all whiny.

Anabelle shook her head and rolled her eyes. "I told you," she said. "I'm *grown up* now."

And then it came. The first sob. Not quite a camel but getting there.

A lot of the noises Anabelle's dad made sounded like animals: his laugh was an excited ape; his nose-blowing a trumpeting elephant; and his sobs—well, she'd only recently figured out what his sobs were when they'd gone on a family trip to the zoo. She and her parents and her little sisters had followed a low-pitched groaning sound, and it had led them to the camels. The guy camel was behind the lady camel, and she was moaning and foaming at the mouth. All the girls in the family were grossed out, but Anabelle's dad got all teary and went on about how beautiful it was that they were witnessing such a raw act of nature. Those "raw nature" noises sounded familiar to Anabelle somehow. And after listening for a while, she realized that her dad's sobbing—when he really got into it, with the deep inhaling—sounded just like the humping camels.

Anything could set him off: an unexpected gift, a sappy film, a finely cooked stew. Or, as in this case, the realization that one of his daughters was maturing.

They hit the Ferris wheel's peak, and there it was: full-on camel.

Anabelle tried to block out his voice and focused on the bloated yellow moon kissing the tops of the trees. Slowly, they passed the pinnacle and started descending along the other side of the circle. She relaxed her leg muscles.

Anabelle looked up to see if Tobin had noticed her dad's noises. But there was no way she could see him from below.

Great, she thought. *Now, on top of everything else, someone who used to like me is getting to see the spectacle that is my dad.*

Her dad took out his red handkerchief and blew his nose: wild elephant. Could Tobin hear *that*?

"Remember when you were a little kid?" her dad asked, sniffling. "And you wouldn't go on all those crazy rides?" He pointed at the roller coaster.

Anabelle nodded. She didn't get why he always had to bring this up when they came to WhirrrlyWorld. As if there was any chance she could forget.

"I had so much respect for you," he said, with a little more elephant. "Even though all your friends would go, you just stood and waited patiently until they were ready for the lower rides. So much inner strength, so much resolve." There he went again, blabbing about her shyness.

Anabelle didn't say anything. She knew by now that if she showed her dad how annoying it was when he got all sentimental, it would just make things worse. And all she wanted was for him to quiet down. But he was still going, reminiscing about her childhood.

Anabelle looked up at Tobin's looming basket. She watched it follow her as they swung around the bottom. "Once in a Lifetime" kicked on, and she started swinging her feet in rhythm with the song, trying to calm her nerves.

When she was finally back up above Tobin, she peered down at the empty half of his basket. It looked so calm and quiet in there. She wished she could press an eject button and magically land right beside him.

But Tobin probably hated her. And he should. The way she'd pulled away when he'd tried to kiss her on the trampoline. It's not that she didn't want to kiss him; it's just that she'd never thought of him that way before. And he'd never given her any signs that he was interested either. But she wondered now, after this summer of disasters, how things would've turned out if she'd given in to him that night. Could it be that he was one of those third or fourth options that Mary-Tyler had been talking about?

Anabelle felt a smack on her shoulder. She jumped, startled out of her daydream. Her dad was so into the story he was telling that he hadn't even noticed he'd hit her. He was gesticulating madly as he carried on: ". . . and that time I rescued you from the big slide, remember that? You climbed all the way up there with those little twiggy legs and we couldn't get you to slide down. Remember?" He shook her arm. "Remember I went up the ladder—not easy on the knees, I'll tell you that!—and brought you down on my lap? On that potato sack?" He let out a long tearful sob, sending himself back into camel mode.

Down below a bell dinged furiously. Someone was a water-gun-shooting winner. Anabelle peeked over the side to see what they'd choose as a prize. But before she could tell, she turned back around. They were at the very top of the wheel, not moving. And she had this awful feeling that they'd been stuck there for a long time.

She put her hands up like before, blocking her peripheral vision. The moon was higher and smaller than the last time they'd passed it. The yellowness was fading, too.

Her dad was on to some story about how they'd hiked to the top of the bluffs.

"Dad?" she asked, cutting him off before he could get to the part when she ran and hid behind a big rock. "How long have we been up here?"

"Oh." He wiped his eyes and looked at his watch. "About a minute. Maybe two?"

"That's not normal, is it?" she asked, her voice timid. "We should still be moving, right? We've only been around once. They shouldn't be letting people off yet or anything."

A smile broke through his weepy face. "Did you only just notice?" he asked, and blew his nose. Major elephant.

She turned her head toward him, her blinders still up. "Yes."

"Wow, you must have something *big* on your mind," he

said, his crying tapering off. "I thought maybe you were actually doing okay with being up here!"

"Not really," Anabelle said faintly.

"Too bad." He removed his glasses and cleaned them with a corner of his handkerchief. "Imagine how symbolic *that* would be! Conquering your problem with heights just before you *plunge* into your life away from home!" He shot his hand downward like a crashing airplane.

Why did he have to be so dramatic about everything?

Anabelle really *wanted* to get over it. She was about to become an adult, right? And what kind of adult couldn't bear to be at the top of a Ferris wheel? Not all those people down there in lines, who'd driven miles to go on daredevil rides. Not kids who'd lived in Normal all their lives. Not *anyone* she knew.

This is so lame, she thought, turning her head back toward the moon. *How can I be the only teenager in the world who can't deal with a freakin' Ferris wheel?* What would she do in college if all of her new friends went to a carnival and wanted to go on the Ferris wheel, but she couldn't? So much for becoming a new person; she'd go right back to being the old Anabelle. High school Anabelle, who was too shy to do anything with bravery or conviction, except when it came to the piano. Or if it was in secret, like the Polar Bear Club.

She *had* to get over her heights thing. And she had to do it now. It was her last chance before leaving home.

She put her hands in her lap and leaned over, looking down. For a second she was fine. She watched the clusters of people milling around, eating cotton candy, holding hands, gripping stuffed dogs, lions, seals. *There they are,* she thought. *And here I am. They're down there and I'm up here. Big deal.*

But then it kicked in. The thing that always happened when she was up high, on a building, a mountain, a bridge. Worse than the sense that she was bound to drop was that unshakable feeling that she was going to jump—as if she were a magnet and the earth was a giant refrigerator. She clung to the metal bar over her thighs. *This is holding you in,* she thought. *It's locked.* But she knew how easy it would be to undo her seat belt, wriggle her legs out from under the gate, stand up, leap, and fall. And fall and fall until—*splat*—she'd be splayed out on the ground. There was a teenage tourist last year who'd killed himself that way. She wondered if his dad had been sitting next to him, sobbing like a humping camel.

She imagined what it must've been like for that kid to

fall that far. Had he died in midair? Or when he'd hit the ground? Or had he hit something else along the way, like another basket or the fence around the ride?

Anabelle clenched her stomach as she pictured the fence impaling her in the gut.

She swiveled back around and put up her blinders, breathing heavily.

"Annie, sit tight," her dad said, rubbing her shoulder. Then he leaned over his side of the basket and waved his arms back and forth over his head, as if he were stuck on a desert island and saw a plane passing by. "Hey, Mack!" he shouted. "Yeah, that's right! Up here!"

The couple in the basket in front of them turned and gave her dad funny looks. She hoped Tobin wasn't looking, too.

Anabelle kicked his leg. "Stop it, Dad," she said between clenched teeth.

But he was only just getting started. "What seems to be the trouble, Mack?" he shouted.

"No, Dad." Anabelle tugged on his arm. "Please don't." She was already stressed out enough, without him making a spectacle.

"We need your patience, sir!" the ride operator called from below. "Mechanic's working on it!"

"I've got a daughter here!" her dad persisted. "Can't deal with heights!"

"Dad!" she said. "It's not a problem anymore—I'm over it!"

"Then why'd you bring her up there?" the operator called back.

Jeez, Anabelle thought. *That guy must think I'm a little girl—like I didn't make the decision to go on this ride by myself.*

"Could you bring a ladder or something?" her dad asked. "Or call the fire department?"

"DAD!" Anabelle shouted, hardly caring anymore if anyone heard her; she just wanted to shut him up. There was no way Tobin wasn't catching all of this.

"Sir!" the guy shouted, sounding supremely irritated. "We'll have this fixed before we can get a ladder!"

"Fire department's always quick!"

"Dad, would you just shut up already? Please?" Anabelle turned around to steal a glance at Tobin. She placed one hand under her eyes, to help her see only him and not the ground below.

To her horror, he was staring straight at her. Well, no, actually, not straight at *her*. Really, straight at her *dad*.

But the look on his face wasn't the weirded-out expression she'd expected. There was a kind of yearning in his eyes—the way Anabelle imagined she looked when she saw a couple kissing who were obviously one hundred percent into each other. That allure of something you want but have never had before. She wondered why he could possibly be looking at her dad that way. What did it mean?

Anabelle must've been staring too long because Tobin caught her watching him. He smiled dimly and waved.

She waved back. Cool, maybe he didn't *totally* hate her guts. She remembered a night, way back in the winter, when Tobin had driven up behind her and honked out the rhythm to the first lyrics in *Cabaret—Wilkommen, bienvenue*—and Anabelle had answered with the rhythm of the next word—*Welcome*—as if they were communicating in their own secret version of Morse code. It had made her feel special and completely in tune with Tobin and she wanted to feel that way again now. Maybe whistle a phrase from something and have him whistle the next part back to her. But just as she pursed her lips, a helium balloon came floating past her head and she looked down to see where it had come from. It turned out there was a guy holding a whole colorful bunch just outside the Ferris-wheel fence, watching the balloon rise. She suddenly became nauseated again, seeing how much smaller the balloons down there were than the one up near her, and she turned back around.

"Annie," her dad said, "I don't see why you're so upset with me. There's no harm in asking for help."

"Yeah, I guess," Anabelle said, facing him. She had only one blinder up, so she could talk to him easily but still keep herself from looking down. "I just wish you could keep this between you and me. I mean, they'll fix it as soon as they can. And all you're doing is embarrassing me."

"Well, Annie. I'm sorry. Sorry I'm so *embarrassing* to you. But you know what? Soon you won't have to deal with this. With me and my big mouth. So maybe you can find a way of humoring me. Just for tonight." Spittle flew from his mouth and a few specks landed on Anabelle's face.

She rubbed them off with an exaggerated wipe. "Okay, fine," she said. "Do what you have to do. Call the fire department if you have to. Why not the *SWAT team*?" She regretted it as soon as she'd said it. She didn't even know what the SWAT team was, or if they had one in Normal—or even a hundred miles from Normal.

She pictured that intense expression on Tobin's face when he'd been watching her dad. Maybe he hadn't been thinking about her dad at all. Maybe he'd met a girl this summer. A tourist girl like Mary-Tyler, and she'd gone back home and he was missing her terribly. Yeah, maybe that was it.

Through the seat, Anabelle could feel her dad's gangly legs kicking back and forth. Her own legs were tucked in, and the vibrations made her stomach feel like a washing machine on high gear. She closed her eyes and listened to people from other baskets calling to the ride operator, demanding to know what was going on. Their calling just kept reminding her that they were stuck, and her urge to jump returned. Again, she imagined what the fall would feel like. Liberating, probably, at first. Like flying. But she imagined that her face would hit the ground before she could really get the hang of free-falling, and it was the thought of the impact, the sound of her neck snapping, that made her squirm the most. Each time she thought of that, she'd say, *No,* just loud enough for herself to hear. A couple of times she even imagined her funeral. She wondered who, if anyone, from school would show up. Would Matt, Lexi, or Jonah? Would Tobin?

Then her dad interrupted her thoughts—hit pause right in the middle of her instant replay. "What do you think of the dark?" he asked.

"What do you mean, what do I think?" Anabelle kept her eyes closed. "You mean, like, am I scared of it?"

"Yeah," he said. "Are you?"

"No, it's nice. Cozy. Time to go to sleep." Anabelle pictured her bed and wished she was lying in it right now. "Why?" she asked. "What do you think of it?"

"Nothing," he said. "Just wondering."

Anabelle opened her eyes and looked at her dad, once again covering the sides of her face. "You don't ask a question like that because you're just wondering."

"Just rolling things over in my head." His Adam's apple bobbed.

"Because . . ." Anabelle widened her eyes.

He batted at the air. "You don't want to know."

"That's why I keep asking," Anabelle said. "Because I don't want to know."

Her dad picked up the pace on his leg swinging. "Fine, but I've never told anyone this," he said sternly, his heels banging into the metal footrest. "Not even your mother."

"Oh. Are you sure you really want to tell me, then?" Anabelle asked. "Maybe I *don't* want to know." What could it be? Was he slipping out to have affairs in the middle of the night? Did he witness a murder? Have to kill someone out of self-defense?

"No, it's okay," he said. "But you have to promise not to laugh."

"Mmmm . . . I don't know if I can keep a promise like that," Anabelle said, teasingly. *Not laugh? There must be something funny about it, then,* she thought, slightly relieved.

"Well, try your best. Okay?"

"Okay. I promise to try my best." Anabelle already felt a giggle tickling the back of her throat. He sounded like a petulant little kid.

"All right," he said, taking a deep breath and lowering his voice. "So I was thinking about us being up here, you know? And wondering if I have anything like your thing with heights."

"Yeah?"

"And that's it," he said, hand extended into the sky. "The dark."

"The dark? What do you mean? What's wrong with the dark? Is it the bogeyman or something? Doesn't Mom protect you from him?" Anabelle cupped her hands over her mouth to keep from breaking her promise, then put them up against her face, blocking out the ground below.

"Yeah, yeah." He laughed a little. With no ape this time. "Not exactly the bogeyman. Just my own demons."

"What do you mean?" she asked. Demons? She'd never

heard him talk about demons. She still wasn't sure if he was messing with her, just trying to distract her from the fact that they were stuck.

There were two deep creases between his eyebrows. He didn't get those when he was joking around. "When I was in the orphanage," he said. "You know, when I was a kid?"

"Sure." She'd heard about the orphanage here and there, but her dad never talked about it much. All she knew was, her dad's dad—*her* grandfather, though she'd never met him—had left early on, and her grandmother didn't have enough money to take care of a kid by herself, so she'd put him in the orphanage from the time he was two until he was six, when she'd remarried.

"Well, my mom would come visit once in a while," her dad continued. "She'd spend the day. Or maybe not even the day. Maybe just dinner." His legs slowed down a bit. "And then, at the end of the day, well, she'd leave. And I'd go to bed and they'd turn the lights out. And I'd cry and cry and cry. Because I wanted her back. And I knew she wasn't coming back." He took off his glasses and held one of the arms between his teeth while he rubbed his face. "And the darkness was just the worst. It was like there was no ceiling, no walls, no other kids. Just me and the dark."

"Wow." Suddenly the sky seemed infinite. Like the rising moon was within reaching distance but the universe around it was a never-ending hole. A hole you could fall down forever and ever.

"Wow what?"

"You think of that *every* time it's dark?"

"Just about. It's always in the back of my head, at least."

"Jeez." Anabelle waited for her dad to burst into tears. This was exactly the kind of story that would normally set him off. But his eyes remained dry. Which for some reason made Anabelle feel as though *she* had to cry. A few tears snuck out of her eyes, and she wiped them away quickly with the blinder on her dad's side, hoping he wouldn't notice.

He wasn't even facing her, anyway. Just kicking his feet rhythmically and staring blankly into space. She followed his gaze to the Big Dipper. Normally, he would've pointed it out to her, and how it led to the North Star, "the Earth's built-in compass," as he liked to say. She still sometimes heard him telling her sisters about how constellations were big connect-the-dot games in the sky.

"And She Was" had just started playing—another one of Anabelle's favorite Talking Heads songs. She let her legs hang loosely out of the basket, into the open air. And just as

the ride finally gave a big jolting *creak*, she started swinging her legs with the music—in time with her dad's—and
they kept it up the rest of the way around.

♪✻

The ground felt pleasantly still and solid when Anabelle
stepped off the Ferris wheel.

"How 'bout some Bop-a-Mole?" her dad said, throwing
his lanky arms in the air as he headed toward the exit.

"Yeah, sure," Anabelle said, lagging behind him. She
wished he hadn't switched back to being his loud self so
quickly.

"I'll tell you what," he shouted without turning around,
"if I win, I'll give you the prize. You can take it with you
to your dorm room. Be the envy of all your new friends!"
He gave an apelike laugh, and Anabelle cringed, picturing
all the brightly colored prize animals she used to keep at
the foot of her bed. She didn't think that would fly in the
dorm.

Anabelle stopped when she got to the exit. She was hoping Tobin would catch up with her. She wasn't sure what
she'd say, but she felt she couldn't leave town without having one last conversation with him. She needed to apologize
for how things had gone down that night on the trampoline,

to find out what he'd even been thinking when he came on to her. Was it premeditated? Or just a spur-of-the-moment attempt? The first step would be getting him someplace where they could talk alone.

She turned around to check if he was nearby, but he was nowhere in sight. *How could he have snuck out ahead of me without my noticing?* she wondered. And then she saw: he was still in his basket, talking to the ride operator. She was squinting into the flashing lightbulbs, trying to figure out what was going on, when she heard her name being called. In Tobin's voice.

"Yeah?" she said, inching a few steps closer.

The ride operator looked from Anabelle to Tobin. "Let's go, bud," he said. "I don't got all day. There's a line here. You leaving, or what?"

Tobin looked down at his hands. "Yup," he said. "I'm leaving." But he didn't move.

Anabelle's dad called out to her. She turned and signaled for him to wait.

"Well?" the ride operator said to Tobin. "Come on, then."

Tobin ran his hand through his hair, then reached into his pocket and pulled out two orange tickets. He looked at Anabelle. "Wanna go again?" he asked sheepishly.

There was nothing she wanted more. Well, she definitely wanted to be alone in that basket with him. But she wasn't sure if she could handle another go-round on the Ferris wheel. She looked to the top of the ride and held her breath, then had to remind herself to exhale. This *was* probably the only way to have a private moment with Tobin; she knew that if she tried to talk to him out on the fairgrounds, her dad would hang around with them, or at least watch from nearby. And then, later on, he'd tell her what a *special* moment that was between her and that Wood boy. Yuck.

"All right, you getting in, or what?" the operator asked her.

Tobin was fidgeting with the tickets, waiting for her answer. He watched her with expectant, rounded eyes, a few corkscrew curls draped over his forehead. Why hadn't she ever noticed how cute he was?

Anabelle turned around and called out to her dad, "Hey, I'll meet you at Bop-a-Mole, okay? In a little bit!"

"Oh," he shouted, "okay!" At first he looked hurt, but when he saw what was going on, he smiled and winked at her. Then he gave her a thumbs-up, angling his head at Tobin. *Oh man*, she thought, *am I gonna hear about this later.* But for now, all that mattered was that she was climbing into Tobin's basket.

The operator buckled them in and slammed their gate shut.

"So, um, hi," Tobin said when the basket moved back a notch.

"Hi," Anabelle said. She was sure she was blushing.

"That's mine." He pointed at the hoodie.

"I know. You want it back?"

"No, you can keep it." Tobin fidgeted with the torn tickets in his hand, tearing little fringes into the edges.

Now that Anabelle was actually alone with him, she wasn't sure she could summon the courage to bring up the botched kiss. She'd forgotten about how Tobin never took the lead in conversations, and a conversation about their feelings for each other seemed like too big a deal for her to get it going herself. Better to start small. "When do you leave for school?" she asked.

"Couple days. You?"

They glided back a little, picking up more people.

"Tomorrow." She looked over at him, trying to figure out if he was sending her any crushy signals. He sure was acting nervous, ripping the sides of those tickets. Was *that* a signal?

"You all packed?" he asked.

"Yeah. Mostly," she said, telling herself not to let her

eyes linger too long on the blissfully kissing couple beneath them. "Still deciding about some clothes. I never realized there's so much stuff I have that I'm just sick of."

"I know what you mean," Tobin said, flicking the two tickets against each other, one in each hand. "It's really tempting to just leave everything behind and start over with new things. Really, all I need is my cello. And some underwear. Not that I'm gonna be playing the cello in my . . ." His voice trailed off at the end there.

Anabelle stifled a giggle and wondered if he wore boxers or briefs.

The ride started moving again; it seemed as if all the passengers were on now. Anabelle gripped the side of the basket, bracing herself for the rise to the top. She didn't want to have to use her blinders in front of Tobin.

Luckily, another Talking Heads song came on—"Stay Up Late." Anabelle hummed along.

Tobin's flicking started taking on a beat. He was doing it in triplets—two sets of quick ones and two sets of long ones, like in "America" from *West Side Story.* Was *that* a signal? Anabelle remembered how she and Tobin had flashed each other knowing smiles across the pit every time the conductor, Mr. Pizzarelli, had to stop rehearsal because the Players couldn't get that rhythm.

She was still humming along to the Talking Heads, trying to decide if she should start tapping triplets on her thighs along with him, when Tobin asked her who was playing on the speakers.

"What, the Talking Heads?" she asked. She couldn't believe he didn't know this song. Sure, he was a classical-music junkie, but, c'mon, it was the Talking Heads.

"Yeah." He scratched his chin with one of the ticket stubs. "I know I've heard this. I just don't really keep track of band names. But you're so good with pop music. I knew you'd know."

"Yeah, I love this song," Anabelle said, letting her legs swing. "It's actually got a great piano part." Her calf brushed against Tobin's, and he quickly pulled his out of the way. Anabelle stopped moving. "Sorry," she said, then thought, *Wow, I guess the triplets thing* wasn't *a signal.* He didn't even want to touch her.

"No, it's okay," he said nervously, shoving the ticket stubs into his pocket. "I was actually thinking when it started, it'd be fun to watch you play it."

Hmm. Now that seemed like a signal.

They'd passed the halfway mark to the top of the wheel, and Anabelle tried to pinpoint her attention on the basket above them. She sat on her hands to keep from using them to block her vision. But the way she was positioned, right up against her side of the basket, brought on the jumping feeling again. Out the corner of her eye she could see the top of a tree. She wished she felt comfortable enough with Tobin to scoot up against him. That would make her feel more secure.

"You okay?" Tobin asked.

"Yeah," she said.

"It's just, you look a little pale."

"The top of this ride kinda scares me or something, I guess," she said. She kept watching the basket in front of them; she didn't want to see the look on his face. He probably thought she was being a baby.

"Yeah," he said. "I guessed that. With your dad up there before."

"Oh, God," she said, turning to face him. "I'm so sorry about that."

Tobin blinked at her a couple times. "Sorry about what?" he asked.

Anabelle had never noticed how long his eyelashes were—like Snuffleupagus's from *Sesame Street*. She imagined they'd feel really soft if they brushed against her cheek. "That you had to see my dad acting all weird," she said. "He just gets overly emotional sometimes. And with me going away and everything—" She stopped herself, trying to figure out how to put it so it wouldn't sound like her dad was treating her like a kid. "I don't know. I guess it's just that I'm the first in our family to go to college or something. It's a big deal to him. But it's embarrassing when he shows it out in public like that."

"Are you kidding?" Tobin said, eyebrows looking as if they were about to leap off his face. "Did you see how *my* dad was acting before? I mean, did you see the whole reason I've been up here, avoiding him?"

"Yeah," Anabelle said, still sitting on her hands. *Just keep looking at his face,* she told herself as the basket rose. *Don't look past him.* "That was pretty crazy. What was he so pissed about?" *God, you know the answer,* she thought. *Why'd you have to ask? Do you really want to hear him say that Jonah slept with Jeanie?*

"Oh, I don't know," Tobin said. "Some woman thing. I don't even want to get into it." He scrunched his cheek, as if acknowledging that Anabelle had had a thing for Jonah.

Anabelle waited for what she was sure was coming next—some snarky comment about Jonah being a bad seed. Something to rub it in her face that she'd chosen

Jonah over him. But it never came. He just gave a what're-you-gonna-do shrug and shifted uncomfortably in his seat.

"Anyway," he said, "I thought your dad was sweet."

"Annoying is more like it."

"No, it's clear he really cares about you. My dad would never be that way with me. He doesn't even get why I'm *going* to school. Thinks it's a waste of time, you know? Like, why don't I just get a job." He turned toward her. "I have to admit, I'm kinda jealous of what you've got with your dad."

"Really?" Anabelle locked her gaze on Tobin's eyes—which she'd always thought were brown but were actually an amazing mossy-hazel color—and realized this must've been what he was thinking when he was giving her dad that odd look before.

"Yeah," Tobin said. "It's like I was sitting up there, watching him trying to help you, and I just kept thinking how I wished I could be a part of your family."

A part of my family?! Anabelle thought. She turned away, not wanting to look at him all dreamily if he thought of her as a *sibling*. The moon was right in front of her—a pearly lozenge among a series of connect-the-dots games.

Wait, the moon was right in front of her? That meant they were at the top!

Suddenly it felt as if there were no sides around the basket, as if the bottom had dropped out from beneath her. She needed her blinders, but she didn't want to use them. She kept her hands under her legs.

There was the pavement, right there beneath them. There was her face hitting the ground. There was her neck snapping. Her nose breaking. Her skull cracking open, her brains gushing out.

"What's going on?" she heard Tobin say. But he sounded so far away.

She couldn't stand it anymore. If she didn't use her blinders, she was going to faint. She pulled her hands out from under her thighs and put them on either side of her face.

And then she felt Tobin's arm on her shoulders and his hands over hers. "Maybe I can help," he said, tapping her fingers. "Here, put your hands down."

His hands were a little shaky and damp, but still, she felt a charge coming through her skin on every point where he was touching her. As if she were her parents' rusty old station wagon and he was the jumper cables bringing her back to life. "Thanks," she barely squeaked out.

She took a deep breath, trying to calm herself down, and

caught a whiff of something familiar. Tobin's shampoo. It was the same as the smell from the hood of his sweatshirt, which she'd buried her nose in some nights to help her fall asleep. The fragrance was cheap and soapy but unbelievably comforting. She was tempted to stick her nose right in his hair.

Tobin's hands closed like shutters over her eyes.

At first she felt lost, not being able to see. But his hands eased against her eyelids and cheeks and his arms into her shoulders and back, and she started to relax. *These are not sibling signals he's sending me,* she thought.

Crowd noises wafted up from below. It seemed as if all conversations had blended into one down there—everyone talking about the same thing in some alien language. She had this feeling that if she and Tobin started talking, they'd be the only ones who made any sense.

With his hands covering her eyes like this, Anabelle felt like she could say anything; being blind to his reaction was kind of freeing. As the hubbub below grew louder and time on the ride was running out, she wondered if she should just go for it: tell him she regretted not kissing him back. Or ask him how he felt about her. Or some combination of the two.

What did she have to lose, really? This might be the last night she ever saw him. So . . . why not?

The Talking Heads song "People Like Us" came on. The upbeat melody gave her confidence.

"You know," she said, pushing her face up against his moist fingers, "there's something I've been wanting to ask you."

"Yeah?" he said. "What is it?"

"It's kinda personal, and you might not want to answer," she said. "So don't feel like you have to or anything."

"Okay," he said tentatively. "Now you've got me worried."

"No," she said. "It's not a big deal. I'm just wondering . . ." Agh! She wasn't ready. She needed more time. But she'd already begun her question. She had to stall, find a new way of finishing her sentence.

Tobin's fingers were getting so sweaty, they started to slip down Anabelle's face.

The voices from the ground were just about at ear level now.

"I was wondering, we're not still at the top, are we?" Anabelle kept her eyes closed even though his hands weren't on top of them anymore. "I mean, maybe I can't see a thing, but I'm pretty sure we've been moving for a while."

"Oh! Sorry, I wasn't paying attention." Tobin pulled his hands away and took his arm off her shoulder, but he left it resting behind her on the back of the basket.

Why couldn't you have just said what you wanted to say? Anabelle thought. Her face and shoulders felt all cold and empty where he'd been touching her. She opened her eyes but didn't look at him. "That's not really what I wanted to ask you," she admitted. "What I really wanted to say was . . ." No, she couldn't do it now. Not when she wasn't sure how he'd react. *If he puts his arm back around you,* she thought. *Maybe then.* "Can you not wait to leave here, or what?" *Ugh, what's wrong with you?*

"Wish I was gone already."

"Me too," she agreed. The basket started to rise and she got a little queasy, thinking about hitting the top again. "People here suck."

"Completely. They're so judgmental."

"I know! It's like, since I'm this quiet person, nobody expects me to be any fun or something. But I just don't feel like I've been given a chance. And then there are things I've done that I feel like I can't tell anyone. 'Cause if they knew, they'd make this big deal about it."

Their basket had risen past rooftops. Anabelle told herself to focus on Tobin's eyes, to pretend they were just sitting on a bench somewhere. Somewhere on the ground. Maybe a piano bench.

"Yeah," Tobin said. "But soon we can start fresh. We can be anybody." He knocked his knee into hers—it seemed like it was on purpose, because his Snuffy eyelashes suddenly lowered and the tops of his cheeks got red. "Who do you think you'll be?" he asked.

Anabelle smiled, trying to imitate his lowered-lid look. "Oh, I think definitely a trapeze artist. And you?"

"The campus slut," he deadpanned.

"That sounds about right," she said, laughing. She pushed her knee against his and left it there. He didn't back away. Which somehow made her feel as though she could finally really tell him what was on her mind. "Okay, so there's something I've been thinking about," she said. She was so nervous that the last couple words got swallowed.

"Something you've been what?" Tobin asked, holding his hand up to his ear.

"Thinking about," Anabelle said louder.

"Yeah?"

"You know that night?"

"On the trampoline," he said.

"Right," Anabelle said. "How did you know I was gonna say that?"

"Because I haven't been able to stop thinking about it." He put his hand on her knee a little too gently—as if he was afraid to put too much weight on her.

"Really?" She barely got the word out.

"Yeah," he said in almost a whisper.

Anabelle wondered if she could lean over and kiss him back right now. As if only moments, not months, had passed since he'd first tried kissing her.

"Oh, hey," Tobin said suddenly, squeezing her knee, "we're getting to that part again." He pointed up ahead at the basket in front of them, which was just now hitting the top.

Anabelle had been so wrapped up in what was happening with Tobin that she hadn't really noticed how high they were. And she was surprised to find that as long as she didn't look down, she didn't need her blinders. But she really wanted to feel Tobin's hands on her again. "Yeah," she said, scooting closer to him, "I'm starting to freak out. I'm getting all dizzy and everything." She wondered if he could tell she was faking because of how calm her voice was. But it didn't matter because he was clasping his hands over her eyes.

She pushed her shoulder up into his armpit and he slid his leg against hers, closing the gap between them.

"Don't worry," he said with an audible gulp. "I'm here."

Anabelle wasn't sure, but she thought she could feel his lips skimming the ends of her hair. Or maybe it was just a breeze. She let her body meld against Tobin's incrementally. She was afraid if she made any sudden movements, he'd back away and it would turn out that she was wrong, after all, about him still liking her.

With her sight blocked again, Anabelle became more aware of sounds. There was Tobin's heartbeat in her ear—louder than she ever imagined a heart could be. It drowned out the pops, whistles, and bells that flowed into her other ear.

Tobin started to tap a rhythm against her closed eyes. He began with his right hand: *bum bum bum . . . bum.* And then his left: *bum bum bum . . . bum.*

It kinda felt like "Do You Love Me?" from *Fiddler on the Roof*—the spring production from junior year.

Tobin continued tapping with his left hand.

Bum . . . bum bum bum . . . bum . . . bum . . . bum bum bum . . . bum bum bum . . . bum bum bum.

Oh my God, Anabelle thought. *It* is! He seemed to be

using his left hand to tap Golde's melody and his right hand for Tevye's.

She couldn't believe it. Was he trying to tell her something? Or just tapping it because it was in his head? Or maybe he thought she wouldn't pick up on it, and it was only for his benefit?

She waited for him to switch to his right hand for the next Tevye part, where Tevye tells Golde he was scared when they first met on their wedding day. And then when Golde's next part came up, Anabelle put her hand on Tobin's thigh and tapped out the thing Golde sings about being shy, right when Tobin started in on the left side again. He only made it through the first beat, then stopped tapping. She wondered if he was embarrassed that she'd caught on. Or glad?

In any case, he picked it up again with his right hand on Tevye's next part. They continued alternating phrases— and when they got to the part where Tevye asks Golde if she loves him and she says she supposes she does and he says he supposes he does, too, Anabelle's heart felt like a cave at dusk, with a whole bunch of bats flying out of it.

They tapped out the last four lines in sync because the two characters sing them together.

Though Anabelle didn't exactly want Tobin's feelings

for her to be those of a traditional old-worlder who'd been married to her for twenty-five years, it definitely beat having him want to be her brother. And she figured the old-world thing hadn't been what he was trying to say, anyway.

"People Like Us" stopped playing and nothing else came on the speakers. It must've been ten o'clock. That's when WhirrrlyWorld stopped playing music on weekends.

The fairground noises from below were so close, Anabelle had a feeling they were near the bottom. She sat there, still not being able to see a thing, wondering what to do next. Should she say something? Should she sit up and kiss him?

"You know," Tobin said, breaking the silence. "There's stuff you'll miss about this place, I'm sure."

"I kinda doubt it," she said.

"O-*kay*," he said, sounding a little defensive.

Oh, no, she thought. *I hope he doesn't think I mean I won't miss* him. Because she definitely would. Especially watching him sway from side to side with his eyes closed when he really got into playing his cello. She wished he'd uncover her eyes so she could read the look on his face.

"Trust me," he said, "I can't wait to leave, either. But there's stuff about Normal that we shouldn't forget about when we go. I mean, things are gonna be really different for you at Oberlin. And this stuff here? It's all part of your past. And that's important. I mean, how can you be a successful trapeze artist without accessing memories from your past?"

Anabelle giggled. "Like what?"

"Well," he said. "This, for starters." He turned her head to the right and took his hands off her eyes. She wasn't sure what she was supposed to be looking at. There was a woman walking by, licking a lollipop the size of her face. She was wearing a tiny little tennis skirt and buggy sunglasses. A lot of those fancy tourist ladies wore shades at night. "Her?" Anabelle asked. "I've never even seen her."

"No," he said. "Beyond that."

"The ticket booth?"

"Farther." He pointed to the side of the ticket booth into the darkness. "Across the street."

"School?!"

"Yup."

"I definitely won't miss that," Anabelle assured him.

"Not even the time Mr. Pizzarelli accidentally threw his baton on stage during *South Pacific*? Or when we all sat around in the pit before *Jesus Christ Superstar* and pretended we were getting in character, like the Players do? Or all those chamber rehearsals when our playing just totally clicked and it felt like we were pros?"

"Yeah, okay," Anabelle said. "I'll miss that stuff. But it didn't have anything to do with *school*." She put her hand on his knee and squeezed, hoping he'd know she meant those things had everything to do with *him*.

"True," Tobin said, pushing his knee up into her hand. He put his hands back over her eyes as their basked drifted backward. "Okay," he said. "How about this? This you won't find anywhere else." He turned her head slightly down and to the left and peeled back his hands.

This time she knew what he wanted her to see. She was looking straight at all the vendor shacks across the street. Bright neon signs flashed: REAL HOMEMADE FUDGE, OLD-FASHIONED PEANUT BRITTLE. OPEN! OPEN! OPEN! "I bet I know which one you're gonna miss most," Anabelle said, laughing. She pointed at the giant glowing chocolate-chip cookie on top of Kooky Cookies, where Tobin worked as a cookie delivery boy.

Tobin tugged on a ringlet of her hair. "What, you don't think it's gonna be Naughty Nibbles?" he said. "I already told you what kind of guy I'm gonna become."

Anabelle reached up and boinged one of his curls. "Yeah, right," she said. "Maybe you should bring some chocolate body parts with you to impress the ladies."

He laughed and pressed his fingers back over her face as the basket floated back toward the three-o'clock position on the wheel. His palms had dried up a bit, and it felt as if they were molded to her eye sockets.

"All right, what else will I miss?" she asked.

He tilted her head back slowly. The ride stopped and Tobin slid his hands to the sides of her face, brushing her hair gently around her ears. "Well," he said. "You definitely can't forget this. They won't have these where you're going. At least not this many." She looked up. The basket above them had moved ahead of theirs. Nothing was blocking her view.

Stars. So many, they looked like spilled milk.

"You're right," she said. "That's a good one." She felt as if Tobin were reaching inside her chest and holding her heart. One little bat was still flapping around in there.

Down below she could hear the clicking and banging of a Ferris-wheel basket being unloaded.

Anabelle kept looking at the sky and saw Tobin's face

in her peripheral vision. He was looking up, too, and still playing with her hair.

There was the sound of a Ferris-wheel basket gate clanging into place. "Well, I guess this is it," she said.

"Not necessarily."

"They're letting people off. Ride's gonna be over soon."

"I know," Tobin said. "But there's this." He took one of his hands away from her head and she could feel him shuffling around for something in his pocket. When he put his hand back in front of her, he was holding a whole slew of untorn tickets. "I was planning on staying here awhile," he said. "I don't really feel like going back home and dealing with my dad yet. You can join me if you want."

Anabelle nodded. "Yeah," she said, her whole body warming. "My dad can wait a little longer, too."

The ride started moving again, cranking them up a notch and into a forward direction.